CRISIS IN CASTELLO COUNTY

The first thing Texas Ranger Sergeant Brad Saunders finds when he responds to an urgent call for help from the local sheriff is the corpse of the public prosecutor floating in the Nueces River. Soon Brad finds himself caught in the midst of a power struggle between a gang of tough western outlaws and a bunch of Italian gangsters, whose thirst for bloody revenge knows no bounds. Brad was going to have all his work cut out to end the bloody warfare — and stay alive!

Books by D. A. Horncastle
in the Linford Western Library:

DEBT OF HONOUR

D. A. HORNCASTLE

CRISIS IN CASTELLO COUNTY

Complete and Unabridged

LINFORD
Leicester

First published in Great Britain in 1998 by
Robert Hale Limited
London

First Linford Edition
published 1999
by arrangement with
Robert Hale Limited
London

British Library CIP Data

Horncastle, D. A.
    Crisis in Castello County.—Large print ed.—
Linford western library
1. Western stories
2. Large type books
I. Title
823.9'14 [F]

ISBN 0–7089–5495–2

Published by
F. A. Thorpe (Publishing) Ltd.
Anstey, Leicestershire
Set by Words & Graphics Ltd.
Anstey, Leicestershire
Printed and bound in Great Britain by
T. J. International Ltd., Padstow, Cornwall

This book is printed on acid-free paper

For Julie

For Mike

1

From the hurricane deck of Blaze, his big bay stallion, Sergeant Brad Saunders looked down on the body floating face down in the Nueces River, his keen eyes assessing the situation.

The water was muddy brown and the current ran fast creating a vortex around the body, for the sleeve of the jacket was snagged on an overhanging branch.

A peculiar stillness hung in the evening air, the stillness which presages a violent storm. Neither leaf nor insect stirred in the oven-hot thickets of mesquite. A snapping turtle lay on the riverbank sunning itself in the latent heat of the dying embers of the day. The setting sun was fighting a losing battle in a sky which looked bruised and funereal giving the wilderness the colour of tincture of iodine.

As Brad dismounted, lightning forked across a mushrooming growth of towering cumulus and the sullen mutter of thunder broke the silence, reverberating like a bass drum roll. An armadillo broke cover; Brad's hand dove for his gun in a reflex action engendered by a lifetime of life-preserving awareness. A creature of the night, the armadillo paused for an instant before rolling itself into a protective ball.

Swarms of mosquitoes had appeared; Brad's thick flannel long-sleeved shirt and buckskin trousers kept them at bay, but he took the precaution of pulling his stetson low over his brow and adjusting his bandanna to protect the back of his neck.

He had hoped to make Roberta, the seat of Castello County, before nightfall. Two days ago he'd picked up a telegram in Laredo from Captain Hall, his commanding officer, requesting him to call on Sheriff Tom Vance, from whom he'd had an appeal for help. He'd come thus far as fast as he could for Vance was a competent lawman who wouldn't ask the rangers for help unless he really needed it.

Brad was looking forward to seeing Vance. After a fortnight's patrol to the northernmost limit of the Special Company's territory, the prospect of a chat with a fellow lawman and a soft bed for the night suddenly seemed infinitely more attractive to roughing it in the wilderness.

Keeping a sharp look-out for deadly moccasin snakes, he waded thigh deep into the river, bracing himself against the current. As he caught hold of the legs of the corpse he was relieved to find decomposition had not advanced so far as to prevent the body from staying in one piece. The sleeve of the jacket ripped clear of the snag and he hauled the corpse out of the water and laid it face-upwards on the bank.

The body was that of a well-dressed man in his early fifties. He was of imposing appearance; over six feet tall, around 180 pounds, with a distinctive mane of silver-grey hair and a matching bushy beard.

Brad had no time for a closer inspection for the storm was closing in. Lightning flickered incessantly, the crash of thunder made Blaze whisk his tail — a sure sign the usually placid stallion was edgy.

The sun was suddenly obscured by a giant hand of grey swirling clouds and, within seconds, what was left of the day had turned into night. Brad cursed. With a corpse on his hands, clearly it was not feasible to cross the river until morning.

The first drops of rain struck the parched earth sending up little puffs of dust as he dragged the corpse into the shelter of a thicket. He returned to Blaze, removed his saddle and brought the stallion down in the open.

As he unrolled his poncho, a bolt of lightning struck a mesquite tree a hundred yards away. The rain was now falling with an intensity which stung his face and hands. It was accompanied by flashes of lightning which illuminated the landscape as light as day. The apocalyptic scene was orchestrated with a tympany of ear-splitting claps of thunder.

When the thunder and lightning had passed, heavy rain continued to fall and Brad was compelled to endure a long and miserable night under the protection of the poncho.

★ ★ ★

Dawn broke with a watery stillness; tattered remnants of raincloud, tinged pink and pale blue, were fighting a rearguard action against the slanting rays of the rising sun.

The stallion was drinking from a pool of rainwater. Brad rose and hung his poncho on a mesquite bush to dry before scouring the undergrowth for an armful of dry kindling and setting about coaxing it into a glowing fire. He cooked and ate a meal of beans and bacon washed down with scalding hot coffee.

'Your turn when we get to Roberta,' he said to Blaze, who was grazing quietly beside him. He patted the stallion's nose. 'Nothin' but the best livery stable in town for you, boy.'

But first he must deal with the corpse.

He wrinkled his nose. It was bloating now. Flies hummed in a dense swarm as he drew near it. Fastening his bandanna over his mouth and nose, Brad dragged it back into the open. His priority was to find some means of identification.

The man must have been on horseback, for his pants were tucked into a pair of fancy leather boots. There was no gunbelt, but in a shoulder holster he was carrying an ornate .38 rimfire Sharps, fully loaded, four-barrel cluster derringer.

A turn-out of the pockets revealed the kind of things he would have expected to find in the pockets of a well-to-do citizen; a leather wallet with several soaked dollar bills, a silver case with some thin cigars, a packet of lucifers, a gold watch and chain, a silver toothpick, a handkerchief, a few loose cents and a well-thumbed, leather-bound copy of a book which, as he clicked through it, he could see was written in a language with which he was not familiar.

So far, no means of identification . . .

But, as he was about to close the book, he noticed that on the flyleaf was inscribed the legend, 'To Dan, from Lee, 1848' and on the inside front cover, the name, 'Dan Castello'.

He walked over to the riverbank. He had found the body a hundred yards from the crossing. The current was moving swiftly, swollen with the previous night's rain. To get the corpse across would be difficult, but not impossible. The only practical solution would be to secure it to his horse, and once he reached the other side transport it on a crude travois made from mesquite branches.

He was in the act of lifting the corpse when he heard the sounds of an approaching rider. Dropping it, he turned and in one involuntary movement slid his right hand onto the butt of his Peacemaker.

He needn't have worried for the rider hadn't spotted him. The girl was riding a splendid roan, heading towards the crossing from the other side of the river. Her attention was focused on a point behind Brad.

Brad turned to see a man about fifty yards away. He was sitting motionless on a sorrel.

The girl reined in almost directly opposite to Brad.

'Hi, Joe! I'm comin' across,' she called out.

Before Brad could shout a warning, she kicked her roan down the bank into the river. Her haste was her undoing. Instead of allowing her mount to pick its own way, the girl forced the pace and in the swirling current, the animal stumbled and lost its footing, unseating her and, to Brad's horror, she fell into the water.

'Help!' she cried, as the current swept her away.

Brad froze. All his instincts urged him to plunge into the river, but like many Westerners his ability to swim was limited to thrashing about in water-holes. He holstered his gun and ran back to his saddle.

He unfastened the thong holding the rawhide reata to the saddle horn. By the time he returned to the bank, the girl was drifting along with the current, flailing the water into white foam and crying for help.

Despite the seriousness of her plight, Brad forced himself to pause and gather his breath before making a cast. He had to get it right first time, otherwise he'd have to make repeated casts with a water-logged line. When he was ready, he sent the loop flying on high trajectory so that it settled lightly about the girl's head and shoulders.

'Put your arms through it,' he

shouted. 'Get it underneath your shoulders.'

To his intense relief she had seen what he was trying to do and complied.

'Easy now,' he urged.

Tensing the reata, he felt the honda tighten around her armpits and he began to haul her in obliquely across the current. She had long since lost her hat and, as she neared the bank, he grabbed hold of her great mane of jet-black hair and dragged her unceremoniously up the bank.

For the next few minutes, she crouched on all fours coughing and retching.

'My horse, is she OK?' she asked abruptly, when the paroxysm had passed and she had recovered her breath.

Brad smiled approvingly. A true Westerner always put his horse first.

'She's fine, miss,' he replied, helping her to her feet. 'She got outa the river OK. Look, she's over yonder with mine.'

He observed the girl as he spoke. Maybe seventeen or eighteen, her colouring was dark, her features raw-boned with a Roman nose. The wet check shirt and levis accentuated the curves of her young body; it was not the kind of outfit in which a mature woman would be seen out riding.

'Thank goodness,' the girl replied. 'Daddy would have been furious if I'd lost Mist; she's one of his favourite mares.' She stared at Brad with the open, frank gaze of youth. 'I ain't seen you round these parts before, mister.'

'Name's Brad Saunders,' he replied. 'Sergeant Brad Saunders, Texas Rangers.'

He looked round whilst he waited for another bout of coughing to subside, but there was no sign of the man she had spoken to.

When she had recovered, she said, 'I'm sorry Sergeant Saunders, my name is Frankie — Frankie Castello.'

Brad bit his lip. This was bad news. The girl was probably related to the dead man — *he might even be her father*. It was a tricky situation and he had need to proceed with the utmost tact.

'The family that gave its name to the county?' he enquired.

She nodded. 'Franco Castello was my grandfather. Roberta is named after his wife. My father runs the FC ranch he founded.'

'You sure took a risk riding into the river like that, Miss Castello,' he chided. 'Are you OK?'

As he spoke he was trying desperately to figure a way of finding out the first name of her father. Was it Dan or Lee?

'I'll be fine. Oh, please call me Frankie.' She ran her fingers through her wet hair in a disarming gesture. 'Everyone does.'

'And who is Joe?'

The girl gave a start. A deep flush spread across her face.

'The guy you just crossed the river for?' Brad prompted her. He looked round pointedly. 'Guess he didn't stay.'

'Right,' the girl agreed.

Brad could see it was bothering her, so he backed off. He had a more pressing matter to deal with.

'Frankie, I have to tell you that I recovered the corpse of a man about a hundred yards upstream from here just before the storm last night.'

'Who is it?' she asked.

When Brad hesitated, she pressed him again. 'Who is it?'

'Well, maybe you can help. I've been through the pockets,' he said slowly. 'An' I came up with this.' He took out the book and passed it to the girl. 'There is a name inside,' he said tentatively.

'Why, this is Dante's *Divine Comedy*,' the girl exclaimed. She opened it and read the fly leaf. 'Its my Uncle Dan's copy. My father gave it to him.'

A wave of relief surged through Brad. 'Was your Uncle Dan somethin' of a scholar?' he enquired.

'It's in Italian,' the girl said. 'My father and his brothers speak it fluently.'

When Brad looked puzzled, she explained. 'My grandfather emigrated to America in 1830, and, although they were born in Naples, his sons think of themselves as Americans. Uncle Dan was christened Danilo, and my father, Lee, Libero.'

She handed the book back to Brad. 'Daddy gave this to Dan for his twenty-first birthday.' Her voice faltered and her eyes widened in horror. 'Oh no, it can't be Uncle Dan . . . '

'I'm sorry,' Brad replied.

'I'd better come and take a look,' the girl said.

'I don't think that's wise, Frankie,' Brad said gently. 'A corpse that's been in water for a while ain't a pretty sight.'

'I'll be the judge of that,' the girl countered.

Before Brad could stop her she ran ahead of him along the riverbank towards the smouldering embers of the fire.

Brad caught up with her just as she

reached the corpse. Mercifully he had left it lying face downwards, for the flies had gathered again in force and the smell of decomposition held her at bay. As she stood, her face ashen, staring at the corpse, Brad had a vivid reminder of the day when, as a boy in the Panhandle, he'd come across his father's body lying on the prairie with an arrow through his back. The subsequent transition from boy to man had been swift.

'It's Uncle Dan, I know it,' the girl whispered. 'That's the suit he always wore to business. He was a lawyer. What happened? Was it some kind of accident?'

Brad shook his head. 'Maybe he drowned trying to cross the river.'

The girl turned and looked wide-eyed at Brad. 'Drowned? I don't believe it. Uncle Dan was a good horseman.'

'My guess is the body's been in the river for at least a day. Can you identify any more of these belongings I found in his pockets?' he enquired, anxious to get the formalities over before reaction set in.

Tears welling in her eyes, the girl inspected the cigar case, the watch, the handkerchief and the derringer.

'These all belonged to Uncle Dan,' the girl said. 'May I see his face?'

Brad shook his head. 'I shouldn't if I were you,' he said gently.

The girl stared at Brad. Her eyes glistening with tears held in check as if dammed by the tide of emotion that racked her.

He waited while the first flood of her tears subsided, then he said, 'Frankie, how far do you live from here?'

She wiped her eyes. 'My father's ranch is an hour's ride south-west of here.'

'On the other side of the river?'

She nodded.

Brad pondered. Roberta lay some ten miles to the north-west which was in the opposite direction to where the girl lived.

'I gotta inform the local law about

16

this,' he said. 'There's gonna have to be an autopsy. Is your father at home?'

'No. He's been over in Austin on business. He's due back today. I was planning on riding into town to meet him.'

'Was your uncle married?'

The girl shook her head. 'Aunt Renate, his sister, keeps house for him in Roberta.'

She watched in grieving silence as Brad wrapped the body in his poncho and secured it to a travois he rapidly constructed from wood cut from the thickets. By the time he was ready, the flow of the river current had diminished sufficiently to enable him to get the corpse across without difficulty.

Taking no chances, he kept a sharp eye on the girl as she made the crossing.

'Sergeant, do you mind if I ride with you into town? I guess someone ought to tell Aunt Renate what's happened. I'll be able to meet Daddy and tell him, too.'

17

'Sure, Frankie, if that's what you want.'

He attached the travois to Blaze and together they took the trail to Roberta.

The girl's clothing soon dried in the rising heat which by midday became intense. Soon after leaving the river they came to a point where the trail forked and they took the one threading north-west through dense thickets of mesquite and chapparal; once clear of the river, the scrub became less dense and groups of branded longhorns could be seen.

The trail became wider as they drew closer to the town and when three riders came into view, Brad thought no more of it until the girl suddenly reined in.

'Oh no!' she exclaimed, clearly apprehensive.

Brad had no time to speak to her before the riders came upon then.

'Well, well, what have we here?' one of the men said. He was a big, heavily muscled man in his middle twenties. He was dressed casually in range clothes as were his companions. All three were carrying a pair of side-arms and were laughing and talking in the careless way associated with an excessive indulgence in drink. It spelt trouble.

'Well, now, if it ain't my long-lost cousin.' As he spoke, the big guy eyed Frankie with a leer that made Brad's hackles rise.

'You wanna watch this randy little bitch, mister,' the guy went on, 'she's a real cockteaser . . . '

'Hush your filthy mouth, Art Castello!' Frankie flared at him.

'Whoo-hooh!' the man replied. His high-pitched mocking cry was echoed by his two sidekicks.

'Hold it,' Brad intervened. 'That's no way to speak to a young lady.'

The man gave vent to a deep belch before fixing his bleary-eyed gaze on Brad. 'Just who the hell do you think you are, mister?' he demanded.

Even at a yard Brad caught the stale smell of whiskey on his breath. He flipped back his vest to reveal his badge of office.

'Hell, Art, he's a Texas Ranger!' one of the men exclaimed.

Art Castello hiccupped and belched again, swaying on his horse as he did so. 'I don't care who he is, he don't scare me none,' he said.

Brad longed to finish this business here and now with one solid punch on the jaw, but he was mindful of his position; it would do nothing for the status of the ranger service in the eyes of local people for him to get drawn into a fight with a drunken loud-mouth.

At that moment, the man's eyes focused on the travois. Even in his inebriated state he could see it was carrying a corpse.

'Who have you got there?' he demanded.

'It's Uncle Dan,' Frankie told him. 'Sergeant Saunders found his body in the river. It looks like he's been drowned.'

'Is that so?' A grin spread slowly across the man's face as he turned to the other two riders. 'You hear that, boys? Uncle Dan's dead. Why, I guess it couldn't have happened to a nicer guy.'

'How dare you say such a thing!' Frankie stormed.

'Apart from which, you still haven't apologized,' Brad added.

The man leaned forward in his saddle and scowled. His hand hovered over the butt of his gun. 'You wanna make somethin' of this?' he said with a snarl.

2

Brad had no intention of being goaded into a draw. He was, however, perfectly entitled to defend himself and in any case he was tired of this unnecessary interruption to what was turning into a long day.

So, without giving the guy a chance to make his play, Brad drew his Peacemaker with a speed which caught his would-be opponent completely by surprise.

'I'm arresting you for threatening behaviour likely to bring about a breach of the peace,' he said.

At the sight of the Peacemaker pointing unwaveringly at him, Castello sobered up. His face took on a sickly grin. 'Now wait a minute . . . ' He looked round at his companions who seemed to have suddenly become so blended into the landscape as to become invisible. 'Say, you guys, you ain't gonna let him get away with this, are you?'

His appeal fell on deaf ears.

'You make your play first, Art, and we'll back you,' one of the men muttered. 'But I wouldn't take on a ranger when he's got the drop on you.'

'Come on, we're wastin' time,' Brad said. He waved his gun at the two cowhands. 'You get the hell outa here, I got no quarrel with you.'

Castello's erstwhile companions lost no time in complying. Once the sound of their horses' galloping hooves had diminished, he stared balefully at Brad. Bullying had failed, so he tried another tack.

'Hey, do you know who my father is?' he blustered.

'Do tell,' Brad replied.

'Art and I are cousins,' Frankie said quietly. 'His father is Raul Castello, my father's brother. They have not been on speaking terms for years.'

'I warn you that if you put me in jail my pa will have you run outa the county and busted back to the ranks,' Castello said with a sneer.

'I'll look forward to that,' Brad replied with a wry smile. 'Meantime, I reckon a night in a cell might just bring your daddy hot-footin' into town. It'll save me a journey and I can have the pleasure of tellin' him what a chicken-head of a son he's got. Now just unbuckle your gunbelt nice and easy and give it to me.'

Castello complied reluctantly. Brad hung the gunbelt on his saddle horn.

'Frankie,' Brad said, 'take my reata and drop it over his shoulders.'

'Hey, what is this?' Castello exclaimed in alarm as the girl did as she was instructed.

'Don't worry, I ain't gonna hang you,' Brad told him, as he jerked the honda tight. 'Not yet,' he muttered under his breath.

'Now just a minute, you ain't gonna take me into town trussed like a chicken,' Castello protested.

'Seems to me I couldn't have put it better myself,' Brad agreed. 'Now let's move out, I got things to do.'

* * *

It was late afternoon when the cavalcade arrived in Roberta. The town lay on a branch of the Texas-Mexico Railroad and they followed the gleaming steel rails running straight as an arrow for the last couple of miles. The town had benefited from the association and the level of economic development was reflected in the wide Main Street flanked by a proliferation of cheap lodging-houses cheek-by-jowl with shops of every kind and a seemingly endless number of saloons.

The town centre boasted a couple of banks and several hotels. The side streets were bustling with people and Brad, accompanied by the girl and his prisoner and with his unusual burden in tow soon attracted attention, particularly that of a man with a broken nose and shifty eyes set deep in the sockets of an unshaven face. Six feet four and powerfully built, he was dressed in cheap range clothes and armed with a pair of Second Model No. 3 Smith & Wesson revolvers with eight-inch barrels. His three companions noticed his interest and closed in around him.

The man's eyes narrowed to glittering slits of hatred as he stared at Brad.

'Who is it, Ed?' one of his companions asked.

'Brad Saunders,' the man replied. 'Now what the hell is he doin' here in Roberta?'

There was the click of a revolver being cocked.

'You want him dead?' one of the other men enquired.

'Save it,' the big man ordered. 'I ain't ready to kill him — not yet.'

A large crowd had gathered by the time Brad and his party reached the sheriff's office. As he swung down and tethered Blaze, Brad ignored the questions flung at him from every side.

The office door opened and Tom Vance appeared. He was a man approaching middle age, worry lines creasing his face, his gunbelt restraining a paunch.

'What the hell is goin' on?' he demanded, eyebrows raised. Suddenly he recognized Brad and stepped forward, hand extended. 'Brad Saunders? Captain Hall got my message then. Am I glad to see you.' He looked around. 'Where's the rest of your boys?'

'I guess there's only me,' Brad said, after the pump-handling was over.

'Who've you got there?' Vance asked, looking at the body strapped to the travois.

'A guy called Dan Castello. I found him in the river.'

Vance winced. 'Dan Castello? Are you sure?'

'Frankie has identified him.'

'Drowned? Jesus, what a way to go,'

Vance flushed with embarrassment. 'Gee, I'm real sorry, Miss Castello.'

'Get down,' Brad ordered his prisoner.

'Christ, man. What have you arrested *him* for?' Vance said.

'You might well ask,' Art Castello said with a snarl. The shock of being arrested had gone a long way to sobering him up. 'You'd better talk sense into this guy, otherwise your life ain't gonna be worth livin'.'

The sheriiff's obvious discomfiture did not escape Brad.

'Shut your mouth,' Brad snarled at Castello. 'I've heard enough garbage from you for one day.'

There was a stunned silence as Brad loosened the reata sufficient to permit his prisoner to dismount during which time a man wearing a neat grey suit thrust his way through the crowd.

'My name is Lupo,' he announced. He was a small, thin man, with a cold unwinking gaze from eyes set in an olive-skinned, clean-shaven face. He ejected his words at the rate of spent

28

shell-cases from a machine-gun, the way they did on the eastern seaboard, but with a slight foreign accent.

'Pete Lupo is my deputy,' Vance muttered.

Brad took an instant dislike to the newcomer as his eyes flicked in a cold appraisal from the travois to Frankie and came to rest on the prisoner.

'I understand you've found Dan Castello's body in the river.' Without waiting for Brad to reply, Lupo continued, 'I just heard someone say you were a ranger. Would you mind explaining just what your business is here in Roberta?'

With the crowd pressing close, straining to hear every word, Tom Vance said quietly, 'This is Sergeant Brad Saunders of the Special Company, Texas Rangers.'

'Why have you arrested this man?' Lupo demanded, without offering to shake hands.

'Best we talk inside,' Brad said.

Followed by the girl, Brad pushed his

prisoner in front of him into the office.

'Open up a cell,' Brad said. When Vance hesitated, he snapped, 'Come on, Tom, I ain't got all day.'

Once his prisoner was secured, Brad said, 'Captain Hall said you had asked for help?' He pointedly ignored Lupo as he addressed Vance.

'I do not remember you telling me this,' Lupo accused Vance before he had chance to reply.

'I guess I didn't need to.' There was a note of defiance in the sheriff's voice. 'I'm the sheriff of this county and I'm entitled to act as I see fit.'

Lupo's brows knitted in a scowl. 'As your deputy, you should have consulted with me first.'

'Oh, come on,' Vance said wearily. 'Raul Castello is spoiling for a fight with his brother.'

'What's the problem?' Brad asked.

'Both men are standing as candidates for the state legislature,' Vance explained. 'Dan supported Lee, he spoke out in his favour.'

Brad glanced at Frankie. She nodded bleakly. 'Uncle Dan moved around the county as much as anybody. Everywhere he went he put in a word for Daddy'

'And now that you have jailed his son, Raul Castello will think you're siding with Lee, too,' Lupo said. He shook his head. 'That wasn't very smart, Sergeant Saunders. Raul Castello is a proud man. My advice to you is to release Art immediately with a caution.'

'I operate in accordance with the law,' Brad snapped.

'You just do as Pete says, iffen you know what's good for you,' Castello shouted from his cell.

Brad took out his Bull Durham sack and rolled a smoke reflectively.

'Look, Brad, this whole business has gotten too much for me,' Vance said. 'I've had as much as I can take. There's big trouble brewin' in the Castello family, I can feel it in my bones. That's why now you're here

I'm puttin' my resignation in.'

Brad drew heavily on his cigarette. 'That ain't the Captain Vance I knew who rode with Jeb Stuart.'

Vance gave a wan smile. 'I know. But that's all in the past. I'm old and I'm tired and I ain't lookin' to be a hero anymore. Ever since the railway came, this town's been a real handful. Upholdin' the law is a young man's game, Brad. By the way, a guy just told me that late yesterday Ed Drogan and his boys rode into town.'

Brad hitched his gunbelt speculatively. 'Ed Drogan? We've been lookin' for him for months now. He and his boys robbed a bank at Two Rivers. They shot the president and the chief clerk dead. Wounded two women bystanders and a kid too. They split up and two of us trailed Drogan and a guy called Nel Kyle. They turned tables and dry-gulched us. We shot our way out. Kyle was killed. Drogan got away. We've heard nothing about him for well over a year. We figured he'd left Texas for good.'

'Nasty business, that,' Vance said. 'Read about it in the papers.' He riffled among a pile of dodgers and found one showing a man with a scarred face. 'Well, you got him right here. There's a reward of five thousand dollars on him.'

'It sure looks like a busy time ahead,' Brad drawled.

'And with this Castello feud about to boil over it's the last straw, so far as I'm concerned,' Vance remarked.

'So you're definitely quittin'?'

The sheriff shrugged. 'My resignation's goin' in pronto and I ain't calling it back.'

'So I guess it's down to me, then,' Brad said.

'I wish you luck,' Lupo replied, but there was no encouragement in his tone. 'Take my advice and release Art Castello immediately.'

Brad's expression set hard. 'I'm not doin' that. He was drunk; he said things to the girl I wouldn't say to a soiled dove. He refused to apologize and then tried to pick a fight with me.'

Lupo stared at him. 'Is that all? Why, back in New York no police officer would dream of arresting anyone for such a trivial thing as that.'

'This ain't New York, Mister Lupo,' Brad snapped. 'It's Texas.'

★ ★ ★

With Frankie as his guide, Brad took her uncle's body to the county coroner's office. The girl led Brad to it by a circuitous route avoiding the busy main thoroughfare. They stopped outside a modest clap-board house in a quiet side street. Whilst the girl dismounted and went to knock at the door, Brad inspected the brass nameplate on the gatepost which announced that this was the residence of one Dr Maguire.

'The doctor is at home,' Frankie said when she returned.

With the assistance of a passer-by, Brad transferred the corpse to the laboratory at the back of the house where the doctor was waiting. Dr Maguire was a young man, clean-shaven, brisk and efficient. He removed his jacket, rolled up his shirt sleeves and reached for an apron.

'Dan Castello? Well, I never!' he exclaimed. 'I was only talking to him a couple of days ago. Do you suspect foul play?'

'Whenever I find a body, it's the first thing that comes to mind,' Brad said.

'Sign of the times,' Dr Maguire remarked briskly. 'Maybe one day everyone will live to be ninety.'

As the doctor commenced removing the clothing from the corpse Brad outlined the circumstances in which he had found it. 'I'd appreciate it if you could let me know your findings as soon as possible, Doctor,' he concluded.

'It'll take about an hour. Stay if you want.'

'I guess I'll pass on that,' Brad said

hastily. 'I'd best go with Frankie and break the news to her aunt.'

The doctor was absorbed in making his first incision as Brad made good his escape.

★ ★ ★

'Daddy's train is due in soon,' Frankie said, as they rode along the street. 'I guess we'll stop by at Aunt Renate's place and then I'll go meet him.'

The house stood close to the Catholic church, not far from the railway. It was a sizeable house, befitting the dead man's status in the community, Brad thought, as they dismounted and tethered their mounts to the picket fence enclosing a neatly kept garden in which roses nodded in the warm breeze. When they reached the door, a polished brass plate announced that this was the residence of Dan Castello, Attorney at Law.

The door was answered by a tall, slim woman in her late thirties. Her black hair was flecked with grey and her nose even more aquiline than that of her niece. She was wearing a dark-blue dress with a fashionable bustle.

'*Ciaou*,' Frankie said.

'*Ciaou*,' the woman replied, as she embraced and kissed her niece. She moved a wisp of hair away from her forehead when she saw Brad. It was a disconcertingly feminine gesture from a woman whose initial expression he had conceived might be of forbidding disposition. 'Why, this is a pleasant surprise, Frankie, I wasn't expecting you.'

'This is Sergeant Saunders, he's a Texas Ranger,' Frankie said.

If she was surprised to find her niece in such company, Renate Castello was too polite to reveal it.

'Please come in. Your uncle hasn't got back yet.'

Once they were in the parlour, Frankie exclaimed, 'Oh, Aunt Renate! Something dreadful has happened.'

Brad stood quietly by as the tearful

girl revealed the tragedy of her uncle's death to her aunt.

'Do you think it was an accident?' Renate enquired of Brad, when the girl had finished.

'On the face of it — yes. Why do you ask?'

The woman stared at him, as if she was undecided as to how to react.

'We could talk in the mornin', if you'd rather,' Brad suggested.

She shook her head. 'There's no time like the present,' she said resignedly.

At that moment the siren of the train wailed.

'That's the train, Frankie. You had better go and meet your father,' Renate said.

Her voice was level, her demeanour calm, her eyes only slightly moist with tears. She reminded Brad of his big sister, Beth. Strong-willed yet strangely vulnerable. Twenty years ago she must have been one of the belles of the county, but life had left its mark on her.

'Coffee?' she enquired of Brad when the girl had gone.

Brad waited patiently while the woman busied herself. He sensed she needed a few moments to come to terms with the tragedy. The parlour was cosy, carpeted, flower-patterned paper on the wall, comfortably furnished with a well-used medallion-back sofa and matching easy chairs. An old long-case clock, made in England, stood in one corner.

The rattle of cups announced the woman's return. Brad waited while she poured the coffee and took a seat opposite him.

'I expect Frankie's told you I am . . . I was . . . my brother's housekeeper?'

Brad nodded.

'And I expect you've written me off as an old maid,' she remarked. 'But I was engaged to be married, once. To a captain in the infantry. He was killed at Sharpsburg.'

A Confederate, then, Brad knew, for

only Northerners called that bloodiest of encounters, Antietam. Why had she told him this? Maybe it was her way of saying she hadn't given up on life — not yet.

'Tell me, were you in the war, Sergeant?'

Brad nodded. 'Ran away from home to enlist with Jeb Stuart. I was with him when he was killed at Yellow Tavern.'

'All this fighting and killing, when will it ever stop?'

Realizing her question was rhetorical, he said gently, 'I'd appreciate it if you could give me any information as to your brother's recent movements.'

'Of course. Has Frankie told you Dan was Prosecuting Attorney for the county?'

Brad's eyebrows raised. 'Now that I didn't know.'

Renate nodded. 'Two days ago he went up country on business.'

'Weren't you worried when he didn't come back?'

Renate shook her head. 'Dan was a very sociable man. He liked visiting old friends. Sometimes he would call and stay overnight at the FC — our old family home, now his brother Lee's ranch. I never worried if he didn't come home for a day or two.'

Brad laid his coffee cup down. 'Would he stop by to see Raul?'

Renate looked up sharply. 'Why do you say that?'

'It seems to be common knowledge that your family is split.'

Renate nodded. 'The Bible says, 'And if a house be divided against itself, that house cannot stand'.'

'The sheriff believes that there is trouble brewing over the brothers' rivalry as candidates for the state legislature,' Brad continued.

Renate gave a sharp intake of breath. 'I warned Dan not to get involved,' she said in a low voice. 'Since Cousin Carlo arrived, Roberta has been steadily turning into a den of iniquity. Dan knew what was happening but was frustrated because no one made any complaint.'

'You are talking as if you believe your brother has been murdered,' Brad said.

Renate held Brad's gaze unwaveringly. 'Of that I am sure, Sergeant Saunders.'

'What makes you think that?'

'Because Carlo Manzoni is a member of the Camorra.'

Brad's eyebrows rose quizzically. 'I guess you'd better tell me more,' he said, as Renate poured him another cup of coffee.

'The Camorra is a very powerful criminal organization with its roots in Naples. They are parasites on Neopolitan society — a bunch of racketeers, extortionists and pimps. My father was a decent man who emigrated to America to earn an honest living. He settled in New York, but nowhere is safe from the Camorra. He came out West to try to escape its clutches.'

'How long has Manzoni been out here?'

'Our cousin arrived about two years ago. He seemed to be a respectable businessman at first. He opened the Railway Hotel and was elected mayor last spring.'

'So the townsfolk must think well of him.'

'Carlo can be very charming when it suits him.'

'But you think he is involved in criminal activity?'

Renate nodded. 'When Dan became suspicious, he warned Lee and Raul that Carlo was seeking to play on family ties and loyalty to further his ends.'

'And Raul wouldn't listen?'

'Like a fool, no. He will live to regret it. But Raul's break with his brothers goes back much further than that. The family split when Father was alive over which side to support during the war. Raul threw his lot in with the Confederates. Dan and Lee supported their father, who hated slavery. The quarrel reached such a pitch that Father disowned Raul and, as he was the eldest son, that meant he didn't inherit the ranch.'

A house divided indeed — Brad had heard of many similar circumstances at the time.

There was a pause as the clock chimed the three-quarter hour.

'Lee is actually the youngest of them,' Renate continued. 'Before the war, when Father was failing, he helped Raul to run the ranch. Dan was the one with brains — he went to study law at Yale. During the war, my father's health deteriorated and he died the year it ended. The ranch was very run-down and he left it to Lee, knowing that Dan had a career and wasn't interested.'

'So Raul came back to absolutely nothing?'

'Exactly. As eldest son, he expected to inherit the FC. Since then, Lee has rebuilt the ranch and Raul established the rival Bar 65. They haven't been on speaking terms since.' Renate's lips compressed to a hyphen. 'Sergeant

Saunders, I am ashamed to tell you that I believe that my cousin, Carlo Manzoni, will stop at nothing to gain complete control of this county, and my brother, Raul, if he only knew it, is but a pawn in his game.'

3

At the sound of approaching horses, Renate rose and went to the window.

'Here's Frankie and her father,' she said.

Lee Castello was a big man, very similar in features to his dead brother, the same silver hair and aquiline nose, but a thick drooping moustache rather than a deep spade beard. Dressed in a well-cut grey suit and wearing a white stetson, he was carrying a side-arm high on his right hip.

Brad helped Frankie to dismount.

Lee looked at his sister, his eyes full of concern. 'Are you OK, Renate? You look as white as a ghost.'

'Lee, I am afraid things are getting out of hand. Will nothing persuade you to give up your candidature?' Renate pleaded.

'Why do you say that?' her brother demanded.

'Something bad happened to Dan, I feel it in my bones.'

'Your sister feels he may have been murdered,' Brad said.

Renate nodded. She laid her hand on her brother's arm. 'Think of your family, Lee. Is it really worth risking your life for?'

Her brother stared at her in surprise. 'Do you seriously think that my life is in danger?'

'Cousin Carlo is openly supporting Raul. You know how Dan disapproved of Carlo's business activities.'

'Be careful what you are saying . . . '

Renate ignored the note of warning in her brother's voice. 'Someone must speak out. It is because they don't that these evil men take over our lives.'

Lee stared at his sister. 'Hold your tongue!' he exclaimed.

'No,' she defied him. 'It is important that Sergeant Saunders knows the truth. Since Carlo became mayor he has brought in his henchmen and through them, he already controls most of the saloons and gambling dens in town.'

'You have no right to talk this way,' her brother said furiously. 'We are family, we deal with things our own way.'

'Not if you run foul of the law,' Brad said quietly. 'I have to tell you that I am here at the request of the sheriff who has just announced his resignation.'

'Tom Vance has resigned!' Lee exclaimed incredulously. 'I don't believe it . . . '

'He doesn't feel able to cope with the situation any longer,' Brad said. 'But I intend to remain in Roberta until I am satisfied this area is under law and order. I presume you'll be taking Frankie straight back to the ranch?'

'Of course,' Lee replied. 'The quicker I get her out of harm's way the better. How about you, Renate? Will you come too?'

Renate shook her head. 'I'm staying here. I'll start making the arrangements for Dan's funeral.'

'If you don't feel safe, Miss Castello, let me know straight away an' I'll be happy to escort you to your brother's ranch,' Brad said.

Lee sighed. 'Very well; I'll take Frankie home and then come back and help you, Renate.'

'With respect, in view of what's happened, it might be best if you stayed out of town until the funeral,' Brad said.

Lee's lips tightened. 'I'll be the judge of that, Sergeant,' he snapped.

Renate sighed and shook her head. '*Mamma mia*, it was never like this in my father's day.'

★ ★ ★

On his way back down the road, Brad became aware that he was being watched.

He reined in and looked about him, every sense alert.

'Over here, Brad-boy,' a voice called.

He whirled round, his right hand

49

moving automatically to the gun on his hip. He stopped dead when his eyes came to rest on a man sitting in a rocking chair on the deep shade cast by the stoop of a small house. His face was concealed behind a copy of the *Roberta Weekly Intelligencer*.

Did he have a gun there, too?

'Still the hot-shot lawman, eh, Brad-boy? Heh, heh, heh.'

Brad stared in disbelief as the newspaper lowered slowly to reveal a face so gnarled and wrinkled it could have rivalled that of Methuselah.

'By the powers, Sam Clody!' Brad exclaimed.

He leapt off Blaze and covered the distance between the horse and the stoop in two strides. The two men shook hands and embraced in a good old rip-roaring Texas greeting whilst the old man's mongrel dog barked and jumped around them.

'Sam, how are you, old friend?' Brad asked, when they were done.

'Never better. I guess I never thought

to see you again, Brad-boy. Always lived in hope, though.'

'Hey now, don't you weep, old fella. That ain't the tough old Indian fighter I used to know.'

Sam wiped his eyes, his face broke out into a smile. 'Ain't no shame in gettin' emotional at my age,' he said. 'I'm retired now, awaitin' for the Good Lord's invitation. I guess I'm gettin' bored with waitin'. You got time for a whiskey?'

Brad couldn't refuse. He tethered Blaze in a shady spot and followed the old man inside the house. As Sam opened a bottle and poured the amber liquid, he gave him a brief resumé of the reason for his presence in Roberta.

'You sure got problems, Brad-boy,' Sam said when he finished. 'Iffen you need any help, you know where I am.'

Brad looked at the wizened old man with affection. He had been one of the original Texas Rangers, the legendary

51

Los Diablos Tejanos, as the Mexicans called them.

Sam had ridden with Captain Jack Hays on that famous day on the Pedernales River when a handful of rangers charged a party of seventy comanches and emptied thirty saddles with the brand new Walker revolving pistol — the breakthrough in weapon design which at last gave the white man supremacy in rate of fire. Sam went on to fight with the Texas Rangers in the Mexican War and, although well over military age, served with Jeb Stuart in the War Between the States.

It was typical of the man that he should be living here quietly, unremarked by his neighbours. Nobody looking at him now would ever believe he'd been as tough as raw-hide, a man who never backed down no matter what the odds, the finest comrade-in-arms a man could wish for. When Brad had joined the Confederate Army as a raw, under-age youth, Sam had taken him under his wing; Brad had learned more about life from Sam Clody in three months than any formal education could have done for him.

'See here, I still got me my badge.' Sam fumbled in his vest pocket and showed Brad one of the earliest types of badges fashioned from a Mexican silver coin. The inscription was worn but still legible. Brad inspected it reverently before handing it back.

'I ain't past it, you know,' Sam said. He gave a wolfish grin as he took down a Winchester from its clips on the wall. It was the very latest model, oiled and gleaming. 'I gave up on the Colt, my hand isn't quite as steady as it was, but I can still hit the ace of spades at thirty paces with both hands on this.'

'I'll bear it in mind,' Brad said.

When he left the old man, with a firm promise to return, Sam Clody stood in the doorway of his house, squinting into the evening sun until the silhouette of the horseman disappeared from view.

'There goes the son I never had,' he said sadly as he closed the door.

* * *

Brad was in a thoughtful mood when he arrived at Dr Maguire's house.

His knock was answered by the doctor's wife. She was a bonny, freckle-faced young woman with her daughter, her image in miniature, peering wide-eyed from behind her bustle.

'Come through please, my husband's expecting you.'

The woman dismissed her little girl before opening the door into the doctor's laboratory. She didn't bat an eye at the fully dissected corpse lying on the table.

'Ah Sergeant Saunders!' Dr Maguire exclaimed. 'Do come in.' He wiped his hands cursorily on a piece of cotton waste. 'I'm just about to write my report before discharging the cadaver to the undertaker.'

As Brad glanced at the corpse,

54

although the smell of decomposition was masked by that of carbolic acid, he felt his guts begin to churn. Used as he had become at a very early age to the horrors of the battlefield, he could never come to terms with the systematic cutting up of the human body.

'Before I pop the insides back, there's a couple of things you should know,' Dr Maguire said cheerfully. 'Come over here and take a look . . . '

Fighting back his nausea, Brad followed Dr Maguire over to the table.

'Now see here.' The doctor tilted the head of the corpse back as he spoke, pointing out a series of blue marks scoring the neck.

'Puzzling, that,' Maguire said. 'There's also contusions on the wrists, consistent with his being tied up.'

With an effort, Brad brought his rebellious stomach under control. How a man could enjoy doing a job like this defeated him.

'Was he hanged or drowned?' he enquired.

Dr Maguire smiled. 'There wasn't enough water present in the lungs to justify drowning. No, the cause of death was a .22 bullet through the head.'

Brad looked puzzled. 'How come I missed that?'

'Because the gun was fired inside his mouth.' The doctor handed Brad a large magnifying glass. 'Look, the teeth are intact. The entry hole is in the roof of the mouth. The exit hole is barely visible — his hair is concealing it, do you see?'

Brad looked and swallowed uncomfortably.

'It reminds of a suicide I attended back East where the weapon was a .22 Stevens sporting rifle. The police were baffled when they found it had been fired but there was no evidence of a bullet wound on the body. In fact it had been fired so close to the temple that the entry hole was scarcely visible and the bullet was actually lodged inside the brain.'

'It wasn't suicide,' Brad said. 'He was packing a .38 derringer. It was fully loaded.'

'Looks like he was murdered, then. Now, I wonder what caused these marks round his neck? They are too general to be caused by strangulation by hand but not enough to be caused by hanging.'

'Maybe he was roped down off his horse.'

'You mean like cowhands rope a steer?'

'Somethin' like that.'

Maguire snapped his fingers. 'Of course — that would square with the slight bruising on the back and buttocks — so it would appear that he was brought down off his horse by a rope round the neck and shot through the mouth.'

'After being tied up for a while,' Brad intervened.

Maguire nodded. 'And as if that wasn't enough, he was then dumped in the river. How does that sound?'

'Not an end I'd fancy,' Brad observed.

Doctor Maguire smiled. 'I must say it's very gratifying to puzzle it all out.'

'Sure,' Brad agreed. 'All I gotta do now is find out who did it.'

The door opened and the doctor's wife peered in at them.

'Is dinner ready?' her husband enquired. 'I'm starving.'

'That's what I came to tell you,' she said. She smiled at Brad. 'D'you fancy a bite to eat, Sergeant?' she said hospitably. 'It's son-of-a-gun stew. I've got plenty of it.'

Brad glanced at the cadaver and felt his stomach churn.

'Why, that's very kind of you, ma'am,' he said. 'But not right now.'

* * *

Brad returned to Renate's house. When she opened the door he could see she had been crying.

'I just stopped by at the coroner's

office,' he said. 'I thought I'd best let you know the result of the autopsy.'

'That's very kind of you, Sergeant Saunders, please come in,' she said.

Brad followed the woman through to another room at the back of the house.

'Can I get you a drink?'

Brad shook his head. He sensed she was delaying for a few more precious seconds his confirmation of what she had suspected about her brother's death.

'I am afraid your hunch was right, Miss Castello,' he said. 'Your brother *was* murdered.'

The woman turned pale and, for a moment, Brad thought she was going to faint, but with an effort she recovered her composure.

'Please call me Renate,' she said. 'It does not make me feel quite so old. Now, tell me exactly what happened.'

Reluctantly, for Brad had hoped to avoid going into detail, he told her the conclusions which he and the doctor had drawn from the evidence.

'It doesn't look like your brother was given a chance,' he concluded.

Renate winced. 'The Camorra never give any of their victims a chance . . . they rule by terror. They are men without any vestige of pity.'

Brad felt his blood run cold. In his mind's eye he saw men who smiled as they slaughtered their defenceless victims; not for them the eyeball-to-eyeball shootout on a dusty street; such men were the worst killers of all.

The woman perceived his weakness, saw the fear lurking in the dark recesses of his mind and embraced him. Her body was warm, fragrant, urgent, but, as their lips brushed, she drew away.

'I am sorry, Sergeant Saunders,' she said, confused. 'I had no right . . . '

'There's nothing to apologize for, Renate,' he said. 'And by the way, my name is Brad.'

She looked at him, her eyes filling with tears. 'Oh take care, Brad, won't you? Dan thought he could handle Cousin Carlo.'

'You sure you're gonna be OK here on your own, Renate?'

'I'll be fine,' she said. She kissed him on the cheek. 'You take care of yourself now, d'you hear?'

Mamma mia, whatever came over me? Renate asked herself when he had gone, her pale cheeks as red as fire.

★ ★ ★

Tom Vance was busy clearing his desk like a man with a mission when Brad strode into his office.

'Guessed you'd be back,' he said with a wry smile.

'You still intent on quittin'?' asked Brad.

'Never more certain about anything in my life.'

Vance looked years younger now the decision had been made. 'My wife died three years ago. Never had any kids — that was our misfortune, but we were happy that's all that matters, I guess. I made a play for Renate Castello, but I reckon she's a confirmed spinster. Now I've found me a widow-woman with a coupla kids and small farm up-country. She'll do, I reckon.'

Brad rolled two smokes and passed one to Vance.

'It's bad news, Tom. Renate's brother was killed by a bullet through the mouth.'

'So he was murdered? Well, that doesn't surprise me. He was far too keen for his own good.'

'Do you reckon this Carlo Manzoni had anythin' to do with it?'

Vance shrugged. 'Could be, but I ain't saying any more than that.'

'Tom, before you go you'd best tell me what you know about this deputy of yours.'

Vance tapped a sheaf of dodgers together into a tidy pile. 'Everything was fine until Manzoni brought Pete Lupo and his sidekicks in.' He drew easily on the cigarette. 'I remember the day they arrived in town. Snappily dressed guys who looked on us as if we weren't fit to lick the dust offen their fancy Italian boots. They tote their fancy derringers in shoulder holsters.'

'So how come you made Lupo your deputy?'

'I needed help. When Manzoni was elected mayor he suggested Roberta needed a town marshal and when I opposed it he pushed for me to take Lupo as deputy. Not long after that Manzoni took over the Lucky Black Cat Saloon.'

'By intimidation?'

Vance looked uncomfortable. 'With hindsight I should have known what was goin' on when the owner suddenly upped sticks and left. Jan von Blank wasn't a man to scare easy, but Lupo is a real slick operator. After Jan left the rest of 'em went down like ninepins before anyone knew what was happening.'

Brad glanced in the direction of the cells. Art Castello was sitting slumped on the cell bench picking his nose, well out of earshot.

'Renate Castello just told me Carlo Manzoni is her cousin.'

'Right. D'you see now, Brad, what you're up against? Now Dan is dead, an honest guy like Lee hasn't got a chance against a guy like Manzoni. Friend of mine who's been over in New York says these Neapolitan guys are the worst criminals they've got. They're real smart operators. When they move into a city back East they take over the labour force, the administration, the law, everythin'. If you don't co-operate, you're a dead man. I know you've got a reputation, Brad, but even a guy as good as you can't handle this situation on your own.'

'Problem is I can't arrest anyone without evidence,' Brad said.

Vance stared at him. 'You won't get any evidence. No one in his right mind is gonna testify against Manzoni and his men.' He glanced towards the cells. 'You still set on keepin' him in here?'

'Sure,' Brad replied. 'It's gonna save me a journey out to the Bar 65.'

'Well, I guess you're gonna be on your own.'

'And we haven't discussed Drogan.'

'One thing is certain, if Drogan stays, he's gonna clash with Manzoni sooner or later,' Vance observed.

'I'll bear that in mind,' Brad said. 'Well, if you're leavin', I guess I'll have to bunk down in here for the night. Tell me, where will I find Manzoni? I think he and I should have a talk.'

'He lives in a suite of rooms at the Railway Hotel.'

'I'll be on my way.'

As the door closed behind Brad, Vance shook his head in wonderment.

* * *

On his way to the Railway Hotel, Brad spotted the office of the *Roberta Weekly Intelligencer* and an idea occurred to him.

'Do you print bills?' Brad asked

65

the guy in the front office after he'd introduced himself.

'Yep,' came the reply.

He scribbled a few notes as Brad outlined his requirements.

'You sure about this?' he asked when Brad had finished.

Brad nodded. 'And when you've printed it, I want a copy displayed in every public place in town. And I want it doin' right now.'

4

The suite of rooms Manzoni had taken over were the most sumptuous the Railway Hotel had to offer. He was a man of medium build with darkly handsome features and had affected a western-style moustache. He was dressed in a superbly tailored grey suit; a diamond pin winked in his tie. Chunky gold rings, emblems of the Camorra, adorned his fingers and a heavy silver watch-chain hung from his calf-skin vest.

At the present moment he was having a meeting in the ante-room with Pete Lupo. Luca Cerioli, one of Lupo's men, was supposed to be on guard outside the door, but his attention was distracted by placing one cauliflower ear close to the keyhole.

'There's been a couple of developments since yesterday,' Lupo said. He spoke in his native tongue, drawing heavily on a cigarette before sending a cloud of smoke billowing towards the glittering chandelier suspended from the ornate stucco ceiling. 'A Texas Ranger has arrived in town.'

Manzoni lit a Havana and leaned back in his chair in front of the solid oak desk. 'A ranger? They've got quite a reputation, I believe.'

'It seems he was the one who found Dan Castello's body in the Nueces.'

'Not before time. I was beginning to think no one would find it.'

'The ranger is arranging an autopsy. After that, he'll be looking for his killer.'

'He hasn't got a hope,' Manzoni declared. 'But we'll have given our disaffected Cousin Lee and a few more something to think about. What else?'

'A guy called Ed Drogan has arrived in town. He has something of a reputation as an outlaw. He is quite famous, apparently.'

'I wonder if these guys are as good

as they are cracked up to be?' Manzoni mused, smoke pouring from his nose and mouth. 'They were always running fantastic stories about them in the Press back East.'

Lupo laughed outright. 'Don't you believe it. They are vastly overrated. Dime novel heroes. No finesse. Always on the run. They're just a bunch of pussy cats.'

'All the same, we'd best keep an eye on him,' Manzoni said. 'I don't want him trying anything here.'

'I'll put the boys on to him,' Lupo said.

Manzoni's teeth showed in a gleaming smile. 'Good. Now we've got rid of Dan Castello, the next step is to tighten the screw on his brother. By the way, what's happening with Vance?'

'He put in his resignation this afternoon.'

Manzoni smiled. 'So he finally got the message. I'll propose you for sheriff at the next council meeting.'

'We'll have to get rid of the ranger

first,' Lupo said. 'He's taken over. After what Vance says about me, I suspect it won't be long before he dispenses with my services.'

At that moment, the muffled sound of footsteps along the carpeted corridor made Cerioli draw back.

'Where do you think you're going?' he demanded of Brad.

'I wouldn't try that,' Brad muttered, as Cerioli's hand slid inside his jacket.

He got no further, for Brad's hand shot out and seized his wrist, holding it in a grip that made the small bones crunch. Brad disarmed Cerioli with his free hand and flinging the man aside, he opened the door and walked in.

'Who the hell are you!' Manzoni exclaimed, half rising from his chair.

'It's the ranger, boss. Sergeant Saunders,' Lupo informed him.

Brad tossed Cerioli's derringer on the desk in front of Manzoni. It was a Model 1877 double-action .38 calibre Lightning revolver with an ivory grip.

'It seems to me a guy's up to no

good if he has to keep a watchdog outside his door,' he remarked.

Manzoni drew back in his swivel chair. 'I don't know what you are talking about, Sergeant Saunders,' he said smoothly. 'I'm the mayor of this town and I'm having a private meeting with one of my business associates. I am a busy man and I prefer people to make an appointment if they wish to see me. I don't like being interrupted.'

'You're gonna have to get used to it, I guess,' Brad said. 'I'm investigating the murder of Dan Castello.'

'Murder? What do you mean? I understood he was drowned.'

'The autopsy shows he was shot through the mouth before he was dumped in the river.'

'Well, I never!' Manzoni exclaimed. 'I was told it was violent out here in the West, but I never expected anything like this. I really don't know how you think I can help you. However, I understand a certain well-known outlaw is in town.'

The statement was made with a

veiled sarcasm which wasn't lost on Brad.

Brad headed for the door and paused. 'There's one more thing, you should know,' he said. 'I'm having some bills printed announcing that from dawn tomorrow no weapons of any kind are to be carried in a public place within the town limits. Outsiders will have to leave their weapons at the sheriff's office.'

Lupo's eyebrows shot up. 'That's a tall order, Sergeant. How are we going to enforce it?'

'You won't have to,' Brad said. 'You may have been Tom Vance's deputy, but you're not mine.'

Manzoni sat back in his chair. 'Now wait a minute, Sergeant, aren't you being a little high-handed? What you are suggesting amounts to nothing short of martial law. Surely such a decision should be endorsed by the town council?'

'The majority of the citizens of Roberta are sensible, law-abiding folk,' Brad replied. 'They will welcome it — they don't want murderers loose on their streets. And in any case I don't have the time to wait for the town council to debate the matter.'

'He's got a lot to learn,' Lupo said with a laugh, when Brad had left. 'Telling the boys to go about without a gun is like asking them to go about undressed.'

'Oh, don't worry about him,' Manzoni said. 'Now that he's dismissed you, what can he do on his own? If Ed Drogan is all he's cracked up to be, Saunders will have his hands too full dealing with him to be bothered with us.'

As Lupo made to leave, Manzoni said casually, 'By the way, should you see Beulah, ask her to come and see me, will you?'

Outside the room, with the door shut behind him, Lupo rounded on his hapless henchman, Luca Cerioli.

'The boss doesn't like employees who don't do their jobs properly,' he said with a cold smile. 'Have you seen Beulah?'

'Why? Does he want to screw her?'

Cerioli's grin disappeared as the diminutive Lupo back-handed him across the face with such force it made him stagger.

'You aren't paid to make comments or to ask questions,' Lupo said, as Cerioli nursed the split lip caused by the impact of a heavy gold ring. 'Find her and tell her the boss wants to see her immediately.'

★ ★ ★

'Come mornin', you're gonna wish you'd never been born, Ranger,' Art Castello snarled, as Brad opened the cell and handed him a tray with a plate of food and coffee ordered from a local restaurant.

Brad didn't even bother to acknowledge the comment; he returned to the office and ate a hearty meal of steak and eggs and apple pie, washed down with coffee. When he had finished he made sure his badge was clearly visible before putting on his stetson and setting forth on a round of the town's saloons.

Playing the tough town marshal was a part that didn't suit him, for Brad much preferred to keep a low profile, but the way he saw it, he reckoned the current situation in Roberta needed a heavy hand. He couldn't afford to have a jail chock full of petty criminals and drunks getting in the way of what he really needed to be about. A good town marshal kept the fringe troublemakers and chancers well under control; that made dealing with the hardcases much easier.

The printer had been as good as his word and the town was already plastered with notices proclaiming the ban on wearing handguns. As Brad strolled along the boardwalk he was aware of an unnatural calm which pervaded the town. Places like this usually became vibrant after dusk, but each saloon he visited — and he was surprised by the number — seemed subdued by normal border standards. Most people knew already who he was, and those that didn't soon knew when they saw the badge which proclaimed his office. Could it be that, at long last, the work of Captain Hall and his predecessor Captain McNelly was showing signs of succeeding in imposing some semblance of law and order amongst ordinary folk in the Nueces Strip?

It was a pleasant line of thought until reality prevailed. No town was safe when outlaws like Ed Drogan were around. And as if that wasn't enough, there was this bunch of sinister Italians lurking in the background. Drogan was a threat Brad knew and understood; the Camorra was an unknown quantity . . .

★ ★ ★

Ed Drogan was one man in Roberta who certainly did not subscribe to the notion of law and order, and never would as long as he lived, for it was twenty years to the day (should he have ever given a thought to it) in San Antonio that he had shot his first man for accusing him of stealing a horse.

Since then he'd never made a conscious effort to live anything other than the life of an outlaw. He was on the run when the War Between the States broke out and had sought refuge within the ranks of the Confederates. Conventional military discipline never appealed to his free spirit and he deserted the regular forces to ride with various bands of irregulars who scavenged off, rather than assisted, the Southern cause. Drogan was a man without any conception of morality and the company he kept as a youth had provided him with the equivalent of a college course in the art of crime.

As a consequence, Drogan had never known a time when he wasn't a wanted man. He had enjoyed that status for so long that no one linked his name with a father who had been a notable frontier clergyman.

Notwithstanding, it always rankled that on that fateful day in San Antonio, he hadn't actually stolen the horse . . .

Drogan was presently sitting drinking whiskey with three of his *compadres* at a table in a corner of the Lucky Black Cat Saloon, the largest and wildest of all the saloons in Roberta, a place where every vice was catered for without stint.

Drogan's deeply scarred face, the result of a sabre slash during the war, far from making him repulsive, made him a fatal attraction to the opposite sex, who fluttered round him like moths to a flame.

He and his associates were joined by a fourth man, Tex Gross, who pulled up a chair.

'Any news?' Drogan enquired of the newcomer.

'Come midnight, Saunders has slapped an embargo on all sidearms within the town limits,' Gross said. Pasty-faced, thin as an edge-on playing card, his

78

long slender fingers fluttered nervously as he spoke. Gambler's hands. Like the rest of the men he was wearing a suit. A match flared as he lit a cigar. 'He's doin' the rounds; he's due here anytime.'

Drogan regarded the cigar butt he'd chewed to shreds with sullen distaste. 'That guy must have a charmed life,' he declared. He spat out the words along with a final shred of tobacco. 'I had him once in my sights. To this day I can't figure how the hell I missed him.'

'Could it be you lost your nerve . . . '

Rick Falcon's observation ceased in mid-flow as Drogan scorched him into silence with a glance. Falcon was the baby of the gang, recruited only recently after wounding a town marshal whilst resisting arrest. Drogan, who had been a bystander at the event, had helped him escape and for that Falcon would be grateful for as long as it suited him.

'Suppose he tries to arrest us?' Butch

Lord spoke in his high-pitched tenor voice. The flesh of his belly hung in a fold over his gunbelt. Lord looked every inch a softie but his record showed a number of killings which would have put several better-known outlaws to shame.

'One man arrest four of us? Come on, not even God Almighty could do that,' Falcon said.

'I want Saunders,' Drogan muttered savagely. 'I want to see him squirm and run before I kill him.'

'He's got a rep,' Gross said. 'We gotta stick together like glue, otherwise he'll pick us off, one by one.'

'What'll we do right now, boss? I'm hungry,' Lord complained.

Drogan leaned over and grinned as he patted Lord's paunch. 'Just bide awhile and you'll be eatin' at the best place in town.'

'We need money. Why don't we just rob one of the banks?' Lord whispered.

Drogan emptied the bottle into his glass. 'Not with Saunders around — it's askin' fer trouble. I got a better idea, Now a little bird tells me that this town is boomin'.'

'Did Beulah tell you that?' Gross nodded towards a woman croupier as he spoke.

The youthful Falcon gave a sharp intake of breath as he feasted his eyes on the woman's dark beauty. She was wearing a red gown with a plunging neckline displaying her magnificent shoulders and breasts.

'God, what I wouldn't give to get my hands on her,' he drooled.

'Forget it — she's outa your league,' Gross said irritably.

'Beulah's real talkative when she's in the mood,' Drogan observed. 'She and I go back a long way.'

Rick Falcon's snigger turned into a silent cry of anguish as Lord's not inconsiderable weight bore down on the toe of his boot.

'Just what do you have in mind, boss?' Gross enquired.

'I mean like gettin' these people to

pay if they wanna stay in business,' Drogan said.

'Protection money. Hey, I like it. We could take over the whole town that way,' Gross said. 'Maybe we could put down roots here.'

'My sentiments exactly,' Drogan agreed.

'Who owns this place?' asked Lord.

Drogan drained his glass. 'It's changed ownership recently. Beulah's in charge now, but the boss, he usually calls in around midnight. A guy called Carlo Manzoni.'

★ ★ ★

The only saloon where the reception was overtly hostile was the Lucky Black Cat. As Brad walked through the batwings, he paused to survey the scene. His sixth sense told him he had arrived at the focal point of any trouble he might encounter in this town.

The atmosphere was the usual fug of sweat, cheap scent, beer and tobacco smoke. A staircase with a fancy balustrade led upwards to the brothel. A big gilt mirror adorned the huge bar with its polished brass foot-rail where the customers were packed for shoulder-to-shoulder drinking. The gaming-room lay beyond and in one corner, a pot-bellied pianist was slumped over his instrument vamping 'Little Brown Jug'.

In a matter of seconds, one of the sweating shirt-sleeved bartenders had noticed Brad. So had Drogan.

As in previous places, tongues wagged and heads began to turn discreetly. Very soon the whole room knew who he was. Brad spotted the guy he'd downed over at the hotel earlier. He was sitting at a table playing cards. A woman, garishly attired in a red gown which displayed most of her not inconsiderable bosom, was standing close behind him, a slim hand resting on one hip, a cocktail glass in the other.

The crowd opened and closed as

Brad shouldered through to the bar.

'What can I get you, Ranger?' the one-eyed bartender asked in an unnaturally loud voice.

'Beer,' Brad replied, and waited while the glass and bottle came sliding towards him.

'I see you ain't displayed my notice yet,' Brad said to the barman as he paid for his drink.

The man's lips curled back in a sneer, revealing a hit-and-miss collection of rotting, nicotine-stained teeth.

'You'd better have a word with the boss.' He nodded towards the woman in the red gown. 'Beulah's in charge here.'

'Hey, Ranger!' a voice called out, as Brad was about to thread his way through the crowd to speak to the woman.

The saloon became suddenly quiet as Brad turned away from the bar to confront the man who was addressing him.

The one-eyed barman wiped the

84

spittle from his blubbery lips on the back of his hand and sniggered. 'Better pay attention, I guess Ed Drogan wants a word with you,' he said.

'Hey, what is this?' Beulah called out. 'You know Mr Manzoni don't allow gunplay on any of his premises.'

'Shut up,' Drogan snarled.

He was pointing his revolver at Brad. Gross, Lord and Falcon were backing him.

'Don't push your luck, Drogan. There's a warrant out on you for robbin' the National Bank at Jansen Crossing,' Brad said calmly.

The outlaw's eyebrows lifted in mock surprise. 'If that's so, then why don't you go ahead and arrest me?'

Which everyone present knew was impossible for the firepower ranged on Brad would have decimated a company of regular soldiers. He cursed himself inwardly for having publicly challenged Drogan. He had fallen victim to over-confidence — a mistake so easily made, so fraught with consequences. As soon as word got round the outlaw had the upper hand, Brad's authority in Roberta would be completely undermined. But there was worse to come.

'I ain't forgotten the day you back-shot Nel Kyle,' Drogan said, his voice blazing with hatred.

Brad said nothing; the outlaw was beyond reasoning with and he was unwilling to add fuel to the flames.

'Rick, go get his gun,' Drogan said.

'It'll be a pleasure, boss.'

The atmosphere in the bar was tense, unbelieving, as Falcon stepped forward with alacrity to carry out the order.

'Now get outa here. Go on, walk!'

It was useless to argue, Brad's only recourse was to withdraw with as few shreds of dignity as he could muster. Without a word, he turned his back on Drogan. The walk back to the entrance was the longest he'd made in his life, for any moment he expected Drogan's hatred to erupt in a hail of bullets.

As the batwings closed behind Brad, the saloon exploded into an ear-splitting babble of excited conversation.

★ ★ ★

Back at the sheriff's office, Brad lost no time in re-arming himself with another weapon. Vance had left behind the usual arsenal of weapons confiscated from outlaws over the years from which he was able to select a decent example of a Single Action Army Model Colt to replace the one he'd lost. Only when he had re-armed himself did he sit down, roll a cigarette and light it, reflecting all the while on the biggest humiliation he had ever experienced since the Confederate surrender at Appomattox.

He had acted as foolishly as the greenest town marshal and was damned lucky to be alive. Never again would he expose himself willingly to such danger without backing. Operating alone had its limitations and he had tested them to their limit.

One thing was certain, he had to decide whether to leave town immediately and report what had happened to Captain Hall or remain and try to resolve matters himself. The ranger boss expected his men to take the initiative, but on the other hand he did not want them to take unnecessary risks.

The sound of approaching footsteps on the board-walk outside distracted him from his reverie. His Colt was in his hand ready, as, after a knock, the office door slowly opened.

'Sam!' Brad exclaimed, as the leathery-faced features of the old-timer came into view. 'What the hell are you doin' here?'

The old-timer entered the office and closed the door behind him.

'I been thinkin',' he said. He propped his well-oiled Winchester in one corner of the office. 'I reckon you're gonna be needin' someone to mind the shop.'

'Mind my back, I reckon,' Brad said sourly.

'Whatever,' Sam said. 'I'm right with you, Brad-boy.'

'Sam, you're too — '

'Son, are you sayin' I'm too old to pull a trigger?'

Brad recoiled at the flash of anger in the old-timer's eyes.

'I just heard what happened downtown,' Sam continued. 'That was a damn fool thing to do, iffen you don't mind me sayin' it.'

Brad took the criticism, tight-lipped.

'How do you know I'm not quittin'?' he demanded.

Sam chuckled.

'Son, I know you better than any man alive. I never see'd you run from no man, let alone the vermin that are running loose in this town. No, Brad-boy, you won't quit. That's why I done come here, to keep an eye on you, d'you hear me?'

Brad regarded the old-timer with undisguised affection. It was just like the old days when he rode as a callow youth with Jeb Stuart. Sergeant

89

Clody was completely without fear, indestructible, a talisman in the face of adversity.

'Could be a big day, tomorrow,' Sam said. 'So let's get some shut-eye.' He sat himself down in the chair and pulled his hat over his eyes. 'I'll spell yuh. Wake me in four hours.' And with that he fell asleep.

5

When the back-slapping jubilation at the ranger's humiliation had finally died down, Ed Drogan said, 'Well, boys, I'm gonna have a hand of monte until this guy Manzoni arrives.'

At precisely midnight, the batwings opened and Manzoni strode into the saloon. Across the crowded saloon, Drogan looked up, caught Beulah's eye and she nodded.

Gross was in the same school as Drogan. Lord and Falcon were playing poker at a table nearby.

'OK, boys, I've had a big day. Time to hit the sack,' Drogan said. Gross scooped up his winnings with a grin. After a few minutes, Lord and Falcon packed in and the outlaws met on the dimly lit boardwalk outside the saloon.

'Beulah says there's a side entrance in

the alley,' Drogan told them. 'Manzoni will be upstairs in his office, checking the takings.'

The four men moved along the boardwalk until it stopped at an alley. Only a solitary cat engaged in playing with a half-dead mouse, paused to watch them as they walked along.

'Let's hope the door ain't locked,' Gross said.

'Beulah said she'd make sure it was open,' Drogan said.

His white teeth shone in the moonlight as he turned the knob and the door swung open.

'You think of everythin', boss,' Falcon said admiringly.

Drogan led the way along the dark corridor until he came to the foot of a steep staircase, the top of which was illuminated by the dim glow of a lamp from the open door of a room.

The racket coming from the saloon below was more than enough to conceal the gang's stealthy approach. They paused at the head of the stairs. The aroma of expensive cigar smoke filled the air.

'OK, boys, nice and relaxed. Let's show this guy who's boss,' Drogan whispered.

Whipping out one of his guns, he kicked the door open and strode into the room.

'What the hell is this?'

Manzoni jumped to his feet, scattering the neat piles of coins and notes he had methodically arranged in regiments on his desk.

'Name's Drogan. This is just a nice friendly call,' Drogan said genially. He eyed the money and smiled. 'Business is good, hey?'

'It's no concern of yours, I don't know how you got in here. Get out.'

'Not so fast, Mister Manzoni,' Drogan drawled.

As he spoke he eased his bulk to one side to permit the others to enter the room. Manzoni laid his cigar in a silver ashtray and paled visibly at the sight of their guns trained on him.

'If it's the money you want, take it and clear out,' he muttered.

'Oh, it's money we want,' Drogan said. 'On a regular basis, that is.'

'What?' Manzoni exclaimed. 'Why that's not only robbery, it's extortion . . . '

'Call it what you like,' Drogan said. 'But lookin' at this set up you got here why, I guess you can afford five hundred a week.'

'Now wait a minute . . . '

'Take what you can,' Drogan ordered Gross. 'Don't bother with the small stuff.'

There was silence while Gross obeyed.

'There's three hundred here, boss,' he said when he had finished.

'Fine, we'll pick up the rest tomorrow.'

'You won't get away with this,' Manzoni said furiously.

'Goodbye for now, Mister Manzoni,' Drogan drawled. 'I can see it's gonna be a real pleasure to do business with you. C'mon, boys, let's go.'

Manzoni was still sitting at his desk in a state of shock twenty minutes later when Pete Lupo looked in.

'I just cashed up at the Rocking Horse. The boys are on their way. Is something wrong, boss?' Lupo enquired.

Manzoni opened a drawer in his desk and took out a bottle of whiskey.

'Something is very wrong.' His voice was shaking with anger as he poured the amber liquid into a glass.

Lupo listened in disbelief as he heard Manzoni's account of what had just happened.

'No man has ever treated the Camorra this way and lived,' he concluded.

'Something must be done,' Lupo agreed. 'Did you hear how Drogan disarmed and humiliated the ranger earlier on?'

Manzoni shook his head.

'By the way,' Lupo added. 'I noticed the side door was unlocked when I came up just now.'

When Manzoni looked puzzled, Lupo asked, 'Who else has a key beside you?'

'Why, Beulah, I guess.'

'I think we shall have to move on this matter quickly,' Lupo said. 'If Beulah is involved, do you want me to deal with her?'

The whiskey rejuvenated Manzoni's lost courage. He pounded the desk with his fist. 'I don't care what you do, I want Drogan and his men out of my hair within twenty-four hours,' he shouted.

★ ★ ★

'Wake up, son, it looks like we got trouble.'

Brad woke up and rubbed the sleep out of his eyes.

'What time is it?'

'The hell with the time. Come and take a look at this.'

Brad became alert within seconds. He rose stiffly out of the chair he had been sleeping in and followed the old-timer to the open doorway.

'Who's this?' he exclaimed, as he

gazed at the figure slumped on the floor. 'Why, it's a woman.'

The old man struck a lucifer to light a lamp and held it as they inspected the body lying face down on the floor.

'It's Beulah, the croupier from the Lucky Black Cat Saloon,' Brad said.

'I heard a moaning outside on the stoop,' Sam said. 'When I looked outa the window I see'd her leaning against the door. When I opened it, she kinda fell inside.'

'There's blood everywhere,' Brad muttered, as he stooped down. 'Hold the lamp closer, Sam. Christ! Where's it comin' from?'

Very carefully, Brad rolled the woman over onto her side. What he saw made him recoil in disgust.

The two men stared at the gash on the woman's face. It went literally from ear to ear, only just missing the carotid artery in the neck. Her tongue was visible through her cheek and blood was oozing steadily out of the wound.

'Sweet Jesus!' Sam muttered in a low

voice. 'Who did this to her? I ain't seen nothin' like that since I fought the Comanche.'

Brad rummaged round the office and came back with a towel. The old-timer took it from Brad and lifted the woman in his arms as gently as if she were a baby and began the task of staunching the flow of blood.

'I'll go fetch the doc,' Brad said, 'and if anyone comes interferin', fill 'em full of lead.'

'You betcha,' the old-timer replied.

Brad returned with Dr Maguire within half an hour. Without wasting a second in talk, the doctor set about the task of stitching the wound.

'There,' he said when he had finished. He studied the unconscious woman with a professional eye. 'We just have to hope that infection doesn't set in.'

'She was a real good-lookin' woman,' Sam said.

'Not any more, I'm afraid. She needs the best of care and attention if she is

98

to recover,' Dr Maguire said, as he put his instruments away.

Brad thought for a moment. Then he said, 'Right, Doc. Keep an eye on her, Sam, will you? I'll be back as soon as I can.'

Ten minutes later, dawn was breaking, streaking the ochre-coloured sky with brushstrokes of red and yellow as he knocked on Renate Castello's door.

'Brad!' Renate exclaimed, as she opened an upstairs window and looked down at him.

'Sorry it's late, Renate,' he called softly. 'But I need some help.'

She was wearing a dressing-gown and her hair was in disarray when she opened the door. 'Please come in. What is it, Brad?'

She listened as he told her what had happened to Beulah. 'She needs lookin' after,' he said. 'Someplace to rest up for a while.'

'Bring her here,' Renate said.

'You sure?'

'I will take care of her.'

Brad exhaled a sigh of relief. 'I'll go fetch her right away. The doc said I could borrow his buggy.'

Half an hour later, when Brad drew up in the buggy, the sun was up, promising another hot day. Renate gasped when she saw Beulah's face swathed in bandages.

'She either can't or won't talk,' he said, drawing Renate to one side. 'I can't do a thing about it until she does.'

'She does not need to tell me who did this,' Renate said to Brad as they returned to the door. 'I can tell you that it is the Camorra. The cut from ear to ear is their trademark.'

★ ★ ★

It had been an eventful night, but so far it had been a quiet morning until the clatter of hooves announced the approach of a large group of incoming riders.

Brad had finished his breakfast and

was just emptying his second mug of coffee. Sam was checking the action of his Winchester. Brad noticed he was wearing his old ranger badge — no one had any greater right to do so, he reflected.

'That's my pa arrivin',' Art Castello shouted from his cell. 'He'll have me outa here in no time, you'll see.'

Brad ignored him. He strapped on his gunbelt, clapped his stetson on his head, opened the door and emerged onto the sunlit stoop just as a large group of horsemen came to a halt outside.

'You go talk to 'em, son, I'm right behind you,' Sam muttered, picking up his Winchester.

Riding a huge roan at the head of the group was a man so out of the mould Brad knew it had to be Art Castello's father. Raul Castello was a big man, grey-haired with a matching bushy beard. He was dressed in a worn brown suit, in contrast to his band of men who were wearing range clothes.

He was carrying a gun strapped to his right hip. Brad counted twenty men in all, every one armed — a tough-looking bunch, more than enough to recover the prisoner if they'd a mind to.

'Are you Sergeant Saunders?' the man asked accusingly.

When Brad nodded, the man said, 'I've come for my boy.'

Brad stepped forward, aware that a crowd of people were gathered to watch the fun. He was under no illusions as to just how crucial the outcome of this confrontation was going to be.

'I guess you know why I arrested him?'

As Brad spoke, his attention suddenly focused on one of the guys in the front rank behind Raul Castello.

He was the guy he'd seen by the river, waiting for Frankie Castello.

'I reckon so,' Raul growled. 'It don't seem much to lock a guy up for. It was drink talking, I guess.'

'That don't excuse matters,' Brad said. 'The boy has a filthy mouth.'

'Now see here, Sergeant. I set out at dawn to come here. Now we ain't goin' back empty-handed, that's for sure.'

'He ain't leavin' custody without he apologizes,' Brad said stubbornly.

'Listen, Ranger, what's to stop me wipin' you out right now?'

'You try it, mister, and you're the first to go.'

Raul Castello looked beyond Brad into the unwavering barrel of the Winchester Sam Clody was pointing at him.

'You stay outa this, old-timer, if you know what's good for you.'

'Don't threaten me, Castello. Your life's only a trigger-pull away. I got a full fifteen loads here and a mighty itchy finger.'

'And if you do try anythin', Captain Hall will move in with the rest of the company — and he won't take prisoners,' Brad said quietly.

With that, Brad turned on his heel. He was just about to close the door when Raul Castello shouted, 'Wait!'

Brad turned back. 'I'm waitin',' he said.

The rancher leaned forward, his face a picture of frustration. His knuckles shone milk-white as he gripped the pommel of his saddle. He was losing face and he knew it.

'You sure do try a man's patience, Sergeant,' he said.

'I got me a job to do an' I aim to do it,' Brad said.

Inside he thought, thank God he doesn't know what happened at the Lucky Black Cat last night!

Respect flickered through the big man's eyes and Brad reckoned he was halfway there.

Raul Castello dismounted ponderously. As he mounted the stoop, he said, 'Whatever, I ain't comin' all this way without talkin' to him.'

'Be my guest,' Brad said.

He let Raul into his office and closed the door.

'What the hell is this?' Raul demanded, when he saw Sam Clody's badge.

The old-timer kept his rifle at high port. 'I guess I ain't answerable to you, Castello,' he said.

Brad picked up the keys and opened the cell.

'Come on, your daddy wants a word with you,' he said to the prisoner.

'What did I tell you?' Art sneered.

Brad escorted him back into the office where his father stood waiting.

'What took you so long, Pa?'

The words died on Art's lips as his father's balled fist smashed into his mouth. His thick upper lip split against his teeth like a ripe tomato, spattering blood all over the place. He slumped to the floor, out cold.

'I should've done that years ago,' Raul muttered. 'Well now, Sergeant, I guess my boy ain't in no shape to apologize. Maybe you'll accept mine as his proxy? You can tell that girl he won't be botherin' her again.'

'OK,' Brad replied. 'I'll release him into your custody, but on one condition — that he stays outa town.'

'That's fine by me,' Raul said. 'He's been gettin' into bad ways just lately. I guess it's high time he did something to justify his keep.'

'Before you go,' Brad said. 'The autopsy on Dan Castello showed he was shot through the mouth at close range. I am lookin' for his murderer.'

Raul stared at him. If he knew anything at all about it, he was a damn fine actor, Brad reckoned.

'I understand your brother was speakin' out against your standin' for the state legislature,' Brad essayed.

Raul's reaction was volcanic. 'Now wait a minute, Sergeant, are you suggesting I am in any way responsible for Dan's death?'

'I have to investigate every possibility,' Brad replied. 'Dan Castello was the Public Prosecutor. You and he were estranged, I think is the right way of puttin' it. If he was campaignin' against you . . . '

Raul's great fists balled and for a moment Brad thought he was going to strike him. The rancher held back as the cold steel barrel of Sam's Winchester pressed firmly against his jowl.

'One wrong move, Castello, and what brains you've got are all over Roberta,' Sam said. 'Just show some respect for the badge. I was wearin' it when you were knee high to a gnat.'

'Take that thing away,' Raul spluttered. 'Sergeant, if you think that I'd murder my own brother to further my political ambitions, then you'd best think again.'

Brad believed him. However, he judged the moment wasn't appropriate to question him about his dealings with Manzoni — that would have to wait.

Raul stooped and lifted his son across his right shoulder in one easy movement.

The Bar 65 hands and the townsfolk were clearly taken aback when the door to the sheriff's office opened and the rancher emerged toting his unconscious son on his left shoulder. Without a word, he stomped over to a horse trough and dumped him bodily into it.

As Art spluttered and gasped back to his senses, his father turned back to the young guy Brad had taken note of earlier. 'Joe, go fetch his hoss. OK, boys, the rest of you go get yourselves somethin' to drink. Don't get your feet under the table, we're leavin' in an hour.'

As he swung into the saddle, Sam Clody said, 'Wait a minute.' He stepped down off the stoop and gave the ranch boss one of the handbills.

Raul scowled as he read it. 'Well, I'll be durned,' he said.

'You and your men are welcome to stay as long as you like, provided you leave all your weapons here,' Brad said. 'As a candidate for the state legislature, you will understand the need for law and order in this town and so I think I'm entitled to expect your support.'

Raul stared at Brad and shook his head in wonderment.

'Well, I'll be durned,' he said again.

Brad waited in his office until the old-timer had collected the Bar 65 weapons. The only one not carrying a gun was the young fellow called Joe. He hung around until the rest of the Bar 65 crew had gone before asking Brad where he had stabled Art's horse.

'Over at Stranahan's,' Brad answered. 'By the way, if you don't mind me askin', are you Art's brother?'

Joe smiled. 'For my sins, yes,' he said. Brad was pleasantly surprised at his quiet manner, so unlike the brash confidence of his brother.

'I see you don't tote a gun,' Brad observed.

'I guess not. It's no use me pretending I'm one of the boys; I'm a student, home on vacation. I've just completed my final year at Yale. I'm waiting for my results.'

Brad looked at the boy with respect. He had a great regard for the handful of youngsters who used their brains.

'When I qualify,' Joe continued, 'I've

a job lined up with a company designing cattle transportation cars.'

'So you ain't interested in raisin' cattle, then?'

'No. Art will inherit the ranch. Pa gave me the chance of an education, so I took it. I believe the days of the big trail drives are coming to an end, in a few years all the cattle will be moved by rail.'

That's the way of it, Brad thought. Clever kids like this are our future, God help us if we hold them back.

'You were watchin' when I met Frankie the other day; why did you disappear?' he enquired.

Joe's eyes widened and his face turned pale.

'It's no use denying it, Joe,' Brad said. 'I saw you. But I was too busy helpin' Frankie to do anythin' about it.'

'You must have eyes in the back of your head,' Joe said.

'I wouldn't be alive today if I hadn't,' Brad replied. He looked at

Joe shrewdly. 'Could it be that you and Frankie are sparkin' each other?'

'I guess so,' Joe replied. He looked at Brad, with an odd look of relief in his eyes. His voice lowered. 'You won't tell my pa, will you?'

'Faint heart never won fair lady,' Brad said. 'Surely a girl like Frankie is worth standin' up for?'

Joe shook his head. 'You can't believe just how much our fathers are at odds with each other. Two grown men, for God's sake. Frankie and I met by chance at a dance in town when I started my vacation. We've been meeting secretly out on the range ever since. If our fathers found out there'd be big trouble.'

'So what's the future in it, then?'

Joe bit his lip. He was a good-looking lad; Brad could see why Frankie had fallen for him.

'Can you keep a secret, Sergeant Saunders?'

Brad nodded. 'If I have to.'

Joe took a deep breath. 'If I pass,

I'm starting work in Chicago. Frankie's coming with me.'

'Eloping with a minor? Come on, Joe, talk sense.'

Joe shrugged. 'What else can we do?'

Brad paused. 'All this still doesn't explain why you disappeared.'

At that moment the office door opened and Art poked his bullet head through. He seemed quite recovered from the battering his father had given him.

'Come on, kid!' he said irritably. 'Shift your ass, we ain't got all day.'

6

Carlo Manzoni was sitting behind his desk in his room on the third floor of the Railway Hotel. The diamond pin in his tie winked in the morning sunlight. His cousin, Raul Castello, dressed in sweat-stained range clothes, shuffled uneasily on the padded chair.

'So how is the campaign going?' Manzoni asked, as he poured coffee into china cups.

Castello tossed back the first cup, wiped his lips on the back of his hand and held it out for more. Manzoni took a delicate sip from his own cup, laid it down and reached for the jug.

'You're going to have to get used to the niceties of polite company in Austin when you get elected,' Manzoni chided his cousin as he poured the second cup. 'I am so glad you agreed to join us. The Camorra needs men of action like you.' He offered Castello a cigar and paused while he lit it. 'Tell me, how is your charming wife?'

'I'm upset about what happened to Dan,' Castello said bluntly through a pall of smoke.

'You surprise me. I thought you two didn't see eye to eye?' Manzoni delicately deposited half an inch of ash from the tip of his cigar into a silver ashtray as he spoke.

'I'd no quarrel with him until he started to support Lee's candidature. True he always sided with Lee but even so, that's no cause to wish him dead. And what's more, the ranger says he was murdered.'

'Very unfortunately,' Manzoni agreed.

'If I could get my hands on who did it, I'd personally string him up from the nearest tree.'

'It's very distressing,' Manzoni said smoothly. 'There's an outlaw in town. A man called Ed Drogan. A very nasty piece of work by all accounts. He may well be responsible.'

'I've heard the name,' Castello said. He rose and began to pace the room. 'But why should he murder Dan?'

Manzoni restrained a sigh. His cousin might have a good cattle brain but that was where his ability ended — however, to his way of thinking, that was no detriment to his becoming a politician. Manzoni worked best with men whose actions he could control like a puppeteer.

'Because your brother is — er, was, the Public Prosecutor. No doubt he had a file on Drogan's activities,' Manzoni said smoothly. 'I understand Western outlaws have been known to burn down courthouses to destroy the files such officials keep on their activities.'

'I'll kill the bastard if I meet him.' Castello's hand strayed to his hip before he realized he had deposited his trusty Remington at the sheriff's office.

'He has a gang of accomplices with him. I should leave him to the law, if I were you,' Manzoni advised. 'It would never do for a prospective candidate for the state legislature to be seen to take the law into his own hands.'

Castello nodded. 'Do you reckon Lee will pick up votes on account of what's happened to Dan?'

Manzoni drew heavily on his cigar while he thought for a moment. 'A sympathy vote? Not if you show up at the funeral.'

'When is it?'

'At noon, tomorrow.'

'I need a drink. You got any whiskey?'

Castello waited while Manzoni poured a nip for himself and a generous measure for his cousin.

'Do you really think I should go?'

His cousin's eyebrows raised. 'But of course. We're all going. We are a family, after all, despite our differences.'

★ ★ ★

In an adjacent, much smaller room, Pete Lupo was meeting with his two henchmen, Luca Cerioli and

Umberto Rocca. The latter was a heavily built man with brutal, almost ape-like features. All three were dressed in flashy Italian-cut suits.

'The boss is upset about what happened last night.' Lupo made his understatement in native Italian. He drew smoothly on a small cigar.

'Was it Beulah who left the door open?' Rocca asked.

Lupo nodded. 'It seems that she and Drogan were acquainted.' He looked at his fingernails with an air of studied concern. 'It was foolish of her to get involved.'

'*Mamma mia*, she was a real looker,' Rocca said, with a titter. 'I'd have given anything to see it when you ripped her face.'

Lupo regarded his henchman with undisguised contempt. 'Women like her are of no account.'

'Jesus!' Rocca exclaimed suddenly. 'Does the boss know it was her?'

'But of course,' Lupo said softly.

'You mean to say he ordered you to

do it?' Cerioli asked incredulously.

Lupo's sibilant '*Si*' carried the sinister overtone of a snake's hiss.

'If Drogan finds out you did it, he'll come looking for you,' Rocca said.

'No doubt he will,' Lupo said with a smile. 'In the meantime, I want *you* to watch his every move.'

'He's got a permanent bodyguard,' Rocca noted. 'Where's he staying?'

'He's living in a cheap lodging-house near Johnson's Hardware Store.'

'What about the ranger?' asked Cerioli.

Lupo's lip curled. 'He is a spent force, I believe.'

'If I see him again, I'll kill him,' Cerioli said.

Lupo showed the first sign of losing his usual composure. 'You will do nothing without my permission. Is that clear?'

'He had no right to push me around,' Cerioli grumbled.

'If you'd had your wits about you,

it would never have happened,' Lupo snapped. 'Another lapse like that and you're off the payroll.'

Cerioli went pale under his tan. Nobody went off a Camorra payroll and lived.

'It could be the ranger lost so much face last night he'll leave town,' Lupo continued. He shrugged. 'But if he doesn't, what can he achieve on his own?'

'So how do you propose we deal with Drogan and his men?' Rocca enquired.

For answer, Lupo rose and went over to a wooden box from which he took out three carbines. He kept one himself and tossed one each to Cerioli and Rocca.

'These are brand new Evans guns,' Lupo said. 'Brought out last year. Lever-action, they chamber a special .44 centre fire cartridge. The military have turned them down — the mechanism is too complex for their simple minds, so I bought them cheap.

I was certain that one day they would be of use to us.'

'How many rounds does the magazine hold?' asked Rocca as he gazed at the weapon with interest.

'This model fires twenty-six,' Lupo replied.

'That ought to be enough,' Cerioli said with a grin.

'I have considered the matter very carefully and decided we should use plenty of firepower,' Lupo said. 'Familiarize yourselves with the mechanism. When we've finished the job, hand them back to me, is that understood?'

'So when do we do it?' Rocca asked.

'That's why I've called this meeting,' Lupo said.

★ ★ ★

Drogan was just concluding a gargantuan breakfast of steak and eggs in the parlour of his lodgings when Rick Falcon appeared.

'Boss, I got me some news,' he said excitedly.

'Spit it out then, boy,' Drogan said with his mouth full.

'Beulah's gone missing.'

Drogan drained his coffee cup with a gulp and set it down.

'Gone missing? She was OK last night.'

'She's not been seen this morning. Her room's empty and one of the barmen at the saloon says there's blood all over the place.'

'Round up the boys and we'll go take a look.'

Five minutes later, Drogan was inspecting Beulah's room for himself. It was a small room one flight up from the office, reached from the staircase at the side entrance. The heavy scent of perfume still hung on the air. There was no mistaking the bloodstains on the bedsheets and carpet.

'Looks like she crawled to the door, down the stairs and out into the alley,' Gross said.

'Didn't anyone hear anything?' Drogan demanded.

'Nary a thing,' Gross replied.

They went outside and Drogan studied the stains. 'I ain't no tracker,' he said. 'But it looks like she crawled downstairs through the door and onto the boardwalk . . . '

He straightened up and looked ahead. 'So where was she headin'?'

'The sheriff's office?' Lord voiced the suggestion they were all considering.

Drogan grinned. 'Well, I guess we'd best go pay our respects.'

From his station in the deep shadow of the doorway, Sam Clody observed the approach of Drogan and his men. He breathed a sigh of relief that Brad wasn't here — he'd gone across to Renate Castello's house to check on Beulah.

'Can't you boys read?' demanded Sam petulantly, taking the initiative as Drogan and his men drew closer.

Drogan, caught wrong-footed, looked puzzled.

'The sidearms,' Sam prompted. 'There's bills plastered all over town bannin' 'em.'

Drogan's great bellow of laughter was echoed by those of Gross, Lord and Falcon.

'Now see here, old man, your day is long gone. Interferin' with us is only gonna shorten what time you do have left. Just tell us what happened to Beulah and we'll be on our way.'

Drogan jerked back with a foul oath as Sam's Winchester jabbed into his belly.

'Ever seen a guy gut shot, Drogan? He don't stop screaming for hours. Now, unless you want to share that experience, hand over your gun.'

'Well now, I sure do admire a man with spunk,' Drogan said. 'But shootin' me ain't gonna save you from a bullet. So how about we call a truce?'

Sam saw three weapons pointing at him and was forced to agree.

'So let's all put up our weapons and talk, shall we?' Drogan suggested.

Sam uncocked his Winchester while the outlaws holstered their guns.

'Beulah came crawlin' here on her belly last night,' Sam told them. 'She'd lost so much blood even a greenhorn could have followed her trail. She's been cut from ear to ear.'

Drogan fingered the livid sabre scar on his own face. 'Where is she now?' he demanded.

'Sergeant Saunders fetched the doctor and after he'd stitched her up, he found her someplace to stay.'

'Who did it?' Drogan demanded.

'We ain't got the slightest idea,' Sam replied.

'So where is she now?'

Sam spat deftly into the spittoon. 'I ain't in a position to disclose that.'

'I want to know where she is,' Drogan demanded ominously.

'If you wait a minute, maybe you'll get all your answers,' Sam said. He pointed to Brad who was approaching along the boardwalk as he spoke.

'I thought you'd have left town by

124

now,' Drogan said with a sneer, as Brad entered the office.

Brad refused to be drawn. All his instincts urged him to exercise his legal powers of arrest but common sense told him the odds of succeeding were slim. On the opposite side of the coin, Drogan and his men knew that any attempt at aggression on their part was certain to result in the death of one or more of them — particularly as Brad was backed by the old timer. It was a classic stand-off.

'I ain't leaving until I've finished my business here,' Brad said bluntly. 'And that includes arresting you.'

'You hearin' this, boys?' Drogan said with a sneer. 'I'm warnin' you, Saunders, next time you show your face downtown you're a dead man.'

'I wouldn't be so sure, if I was you,' Brad said. 'The Camorra might get you first.'

'The *who*?'

'The Camorra — it's an Italian criminal organization that's trying to take over this town.'

'What the hell are you talkin' about?' Drogan demanded.

'C'mon, boss, we're wastin' time,' Gross said. 'He don't know nothin'.'

'OK, let's go,' Drogan concurred. As they walked in a tight group back across the street, Gross said, 'We didn't find out where the ranger hid Beulah, did we?'

'I don't think we need her,' Drogan said. 'It has to be down to Manzoni. He must have figured out that Beulah left the door on the latch.'

'That little shit ain't capable of cutting himself with a razor,' Lord said flatly.

'Maybe not,' Gross replied. 'But Beulah said he had a sidekick called Pete Lupo. Maybe we should check him out.'

'Hey, wait a minute!' Lord exclaimed. 'Manzoni, Lupo, ain't they all Italian names?'

'So what?' Drogan demanded.

'Could be they belong to this

Camorra the ranger was talkin' about.'

'Aw shut up,' Drogan snarled. 'As far as I'm concerned they're just another bunch of foreign Nancy-boys.'

★ ★ ★

'Sooner or later, they'll figure out it was Pete Lupo and I wish them all the luck in the world,' Brad remarked to Sam, as he watched the retreating backs of the outlaw gang.

'Was it Lupo who did that to Beulah?' Sam demanded.

Brad shook his head. 'She was too frightened to talk. But Miss Castello thinks it was Lupo or one of his men.'

'How's that?'

'Because apparently that's how the Camorra operate. They always cut their victims from ear to ear.'

Sam spat into the spittoon. 'Hell's teeth and we called the Comanches uncivilized. Brad-boy, if I read this situation correctly then I opine you'd best be pinnin' your hopes on Lupo and Drogan blowing each other to hell and then go pick up the pieces.'

Which was sound advice, Brad was forced to concede.

'Meantime I got me a problem,' he said. 'I don't know why the Camorra did it.'

* * *

Over the years, Brad had become adept at sensing the atmosphere of a town. Daily life in Roberta was proceeding with the uneasy calm of a wagon-train expecting an assault by Indians. Renate had told him Dan Castello's funeral was planned for noon tomorrow. Lee Castello and his family were coming — and so was his estranged brother, for Raul had told Sam so when he and his men collected their weapons and left town.

Roberta was a typical border town where nothing happened without someone noticing and news spread with the speed of a prairie fire. The fact that Brad hadn't left and was continuing to operate his gun embargo was noted, particularly when a man as big as Raul Castello obeyed it. The only men who contravened the embargo were Lupo and his men, who kept their weapons concealed about their persons and Drogan and his gang who flaunted theirs on belted hips with typical outlaw bravado.

In the meantime, Brad had other things on his mind. While Drogan and Lupo and their men were circling each other like dogs spoiling for a fight, he had need to do more work on finding the identity of Dan Castello's killer. He had a strong suspicion it was either Lupo or one of his men, but what puzzled him was the rope marks on the victim's neck and wrists. The latter was consistent with him being tied up but how could that have happened when it was more than likely none of the city-bred Italians could even ride a horse let alone throw a rope accurately enough to bring a man down off one?

Brad felt the need to probe further. While Sam was managing the office, registering the weapons of incoming people with commendable efficiency, it gave him the opportunity to follow up one or two ideas.

His first call was at Stranahan's — the livery stable where he kept Blaze.

'Tell me, does Manzoni or any of his men own a horse?' he enquired of Isaac Tolley, the head groom.

The guy laughed, displaying a set of false teeth and prominent gums, remarkably similar to those of the animals he tended.

'No — why I guess none of them Eastern guys can fork a saddle. When any of 'em have any business outa town, they hire a buggy.'

'From here?'

'Where else? We're the only outfit in Roberta which does carriage hire.'

'Do you provide the driver?'

'Sure.' He pointed to a man polishing

a hearse. 'Jim Monks. He'll be driving that at the funeral tomorrow.'

'Have you hired any transport out to Manzoni or his men recently.'

'Come with me and I'll go check the book.'

Brad followed Tolley into a small office where he opened a ledger filled with neat spidery script.

Tolley ran his finger down the page until it came to a stop. 'Four days ago,' he said. 'Mr Lupo hired a buggy to go out to the Bar 65.'

'Did Jim Monks drive it?'

'Yep.' Tolley shoved his head out of the office window and bawled, 'Jim!

'Sergeant Saunders wants a word with you,' Tolley said when the man came over. 'Use my office. I'll go check the roan that's gone lame.'

Jim Monks was a young fellow, red-haired, keen-eyed, interested.

'Funny you should ask,' he said, when Brad questioned him about the hiring. 'Mr Lupo asked me to drive him out to the Bar 65. About halfway

131

there, we met up with Art Castello. Mr Lupo told me to wait, Castello took Mr Lupo up on the saddle behind him and the two of them left me high and dry on the trail for about an hour. I'd just given them up when they came back.'

'And you brought Lupo back to town?'

'That's right,' Jim said.

'Jim, you've been mighty helpful. Would you be prepared to testify in court as to what you've just said?'

'Sure, no problem,' the young fellow said. He grinned. 'I heard about what happened at the Lucky Black Cat last night. Folks were sayin' you'd quit but I told 'em no way. No ranger ever quits when the chips are down, ain't that right, Sergeant Saunders?'

Brad nodded, heartened by the young man's infectious enthusiasm.

'Say, Sergeant Saunders, I hope you don't think I'm bein' forward, but d'you reckon the rangers could have a use for me?' Jim asked earnestly. 'It sure gets mighty monotonous workin' here in this livery.'

'We'll talk about it later,' Brad said kindly. 'Meantime, saddle my horse.'

'Sure thing, Sergeant Saunders.'

A few minutes later Brad left the livery stable riding Blaze. He stopped by at the sheriff's office to have a word with Sam.

'How long will it take me to ride out to the Bar 65?' he asked the old-timer.

'About three hours, I guess.'

Following the old-timer's directions, Brad kept Blaze going at a steady canter, eating up the miles along a trail winding through dense thickets of mesquite. At first it ran beside the gleaming rail tracks, later it followed the river until he came to the places where the trail forked. The right hand led to the FC, the left forded the river and continued to the Bar 65 for, as Sam had explained, the river formed a natural boundary between the ranches.

After another hour, Brad was aware that he must be close to the crossing where he had found the body. Mindful that he had never properly inspected the area, he cut through the brush, keeping his eyes skinned for any scraps of material that might just be a pointer as to where Dan Castello had been ambushed — for Brad was certain that was what had happened. He had no luck, the heavy rainstorm had washed the area clean.

He was about to return to the trail when he heard the sound of voices.

Dismounting with care, he haltered Blaze to a mesquite tree and crept forward as stealthily as an Indian.

As he neared the riverbank, the voices became louder, one male, one female. As he parted the branches of a bush he saw it was Frankie and Joe. They were standing on the Bar 65 side of the river not far from where their uncle's body had been found. Their knee-haltered horses were grazing nearby.

Had the conversation been amorous, Brad would have withdrawn discreetly, for he was no voyeur, but when Frankie said, 'Why did you ride off like that?' in a voice that was anything but tender, his interest was aroused and he waited, listening intently.

'When I saw the ranger with the body, I guess I just spooked and ran,' Joe said lamely.

'You spooked and ran?' Frankie said furiously. 'What about me?'

'I guess I just wasn't thinking straight,' Joe said.

'With all your education?' Frankie said scornfully. 'Did you think the ranger might accuse you of murderin' Uncle Dan?'

'No, I was more concerned he'd find out about us.'

'Why? Are you ashamed of it?'

'Frankie, you're being irrational.'

'Irrational? Don't use your clever words with me. What did the ranger say to you this mornin'?'

'He wanted to know why I rode off, so I told him about us.'

'You did — what?'

'What else could I do? If I'd been more evasive he could have accused me of murdering Uncle Dan.'

As the couple were talking, Brad became aware that their conversation was being listened to by a third party for almost exactly opposite, he saw the bushes twitching.

'I hope you had this conversation with the ranger in private,' Frankie said.

'Of course,' Joe replied. 'Believe me, Frankie, no one else knows about you and me except the ranger and I'm sure he'll be discreet.'

'Someone else knows about it now,' a voice growled from the undergrowth, and Brad watched as Art Castello emerged, a triumphant look on his face.

7

'So this is what you've been up to?' Art Castello said with a leer. 'Pa said you had a habit of disappearin'.'

Brad held back as Art Castello drew closer to the couple.

'Purty little thing, ain't she?' Art stared at Frankie.

'So how did you get out of jail?' Brad held his breath as Frankie baited him. 'Did you finally apologize for those insulting things you said about me yesterday?'

'What exactly did he say about you, Frankie?' Joe asked.

When she told him, Art threw his head back and laughed; Joe's face turned white with anger.

'You had no right to speak to Frankie that way,' he said angrily. 'You're a disgrace to the family, Art.'

'Now wait a minute . . . ' — from

his hiding place Brad saw the warning signs as Art's fists began to ball — 'just what do you think you're playin' at, Joe?' Art demanded. 'There's no way Pa's gonna wear it when he finds out you're sparkin' *her*.'

'It's none of your business,' Joe replied stoutly.

'Oh, but it is. Pa's set his heart on a seat in the legislature. You gettin' involved with this little bitch is gonna cause a heap of trouble.'

'What?' Joe cried.

'No!' Frankie screamed, as Joe flew at his brother.

Art laughed and met his rush with a punch on the jaw that sounded like the slap of a butcher's cleaver on a side of beef. Joe dropped in a heap, out cold.

'There was no need to hit him as hard as that.' Frankie was distressed as she ran over to Joe's prostrate body.

Art caught her by the arm, his eyes glistening with a predatory light.

'Well now, honey, now your college

boy's out of the way, maybe I can show you a thing or two.'

Frankie screamed as Art drew her close to him.

'OK, that's enough,' Brad said, as he burst out of the thicket, gun in hand.

Art flung the girl aside and faced Brad with a sneer.

'Do you always hide behind a gun, Ranger? After what Drogan did last night I'm surprised you dare still show your face in these parts anymore.'

Brad's lips tightened. This sneering reference to an episode he preferred to forget brought out a primeval urge inside him.

'OK, if that's the way you want it,' he said.

Art Castello's eyes lit up when he saw Brad unhitch his gunbelt and hand it to the girl. He did the same himself and rubbed his big hands together in anticipation.

'Well now, Ranger, I'm gonna give you somethin' to remember me by.

An' then maybe you'll learn to leave me alone.'

Frankie bent down over the still unconscious Joe as the two men circled. They were a good match for height and weight, but Art was ten years younger. Fear brought the rancid taste of bile into her mouth. Would the ranger be quick enough and smart enough to avoid a beating? If he lost, the consequences did not bear thinking about. But although she had a good opportunity to escape, Frankie would not entertain the idea of leaving Joe.

Brad made the first move, ducking inside Castello's guard to land a punch solidly on the younger man's ribcage making him grunt with pain. Castello responded with a couple of wild haymakers which Brad easily avoided before flinging an accurate punch which split his opponent's nose.

The resulting spurt of blood incensed Castello to the point of losing his temper. He uttered a vile oath and surged forward with a volley of punches.

One of his next flurry caught Brad on the side of the head with stunning force, dropping him onto his right knee.

With a shout of triumph, Castello lunged forward aiming a kick at Brad's head which would have killed him outright if it had found its mark. Brad saw it coming and moved his head to one side. The rowel on Castello's spur raked his cheek, drawing a trickle of blood.

Missing his target threw Castello off balance and he blundered forward. When he turned round, Brad had found his feet again and strength enough to hit him hard under the heart.

Gasping for breath, Castello stumbled towards Frankie. The girl failed to realize his intention until it was too late. With a hoarse cry of triumph, Castello seized her and recovered his weapon.

Brad paused for a moment. Then he said, 'What are you gonna do, Art? Put a bullet through my mouth, the same as Lupo did to your uncle?'

'Why not?' Art said thickly. He pawed at the blood still streaming from his nose. 'And then I'll dump you straight into the river . . . '

Frankie was aghast. 'You mean to say you were a party to the murder of our uncle?' She struggled wildly, but Art's grasp held firm.

Behind Castello, Brad saw Joe showing signs of coming round. His only chance lay in keeping Castello talking.

'You *were* a party to it, weren't you, Art?' Brad said. 'Your uncle was speaking out against your father so well he was ruinin' his chance of getting elected to the state legislature.'

Art's face broke into a bloodstained smile. 'Mr Manzoni reckoned Uncle Dan was way outa line. But just how the hell did you figure it out?'

Joe was almost fully alert now. Brad saw him begin to crawl towards his brother.

'The autopsy showed your uncle was shot through the mouth with a small

142

calibre bullet,' Brad said. 'Probably from a derringer — the kind of weapon packed by Lupo and his boys. My guess is you kidnapped your uncle and held him someplace while you sent for Lupo. He hired a buggy to bring him along this trail, maybe not far from here. The driver testified you met with him and then came back half an hour later. During that time you must have led Lupo to the place where you were holdin' your uncle. I bet Lupo took his time before he shot him, and then you dumped him in the river.'

'I figured Lupo just wanted to warn Uncle Dan off,' Art growled. 'I guess you're real smart, Ranger. Pity you ain't gonna live to see this through.'

As Art raised his gun, Joe rose unsteadily to his feet and flung himself at his brother, knocking him off balance. Frankie seized her chance to spring clear from Art's grasp. At the same instant Brad ducked low and dove forward, feeling the hot wind of a bullet as Art's gun discharged. Brad's headlong charge caught Art straight in the midriff and the two men went down in a flailing heap.

Art was still holding the gun and fought desperately to keep it. Brad seized the arm holding it in both hands and wrenched it back ruthlessly until Art howled with pain and dropped the weapon. Within seconds, Brad had Art face down and had pulled his vest back over his arms, effectively immobilizing him.

'You got a rope?' Brad asked of the other two.

Frankie nodded and went over to Joe's horse, returning a few minutes later. Brad lost no time in trussing up his prisoner.

'You're under arrest, Castello,' he said, when he had finished. 'And this time, I promise your daddy isn't gonna say he's sorry for you.'

Frankie was holding on to Joe when Brad returned with Blaze.

'Help me get him on to his horse,' he

ordered the couple and they hastened to comply.

'Are you two gonna be all right?' Brad asked.

'Sure,' Frankie said. Joe nodded, a bleak look in his eyes.

'I'm afraid it looks as though your secret is out,' Brad said.

'And when your fathers find out, the pair of you are through,' Art said thickly.

'There is no need for them to find out, if you don't say anything,' Joe said.

'Why should I do you a favour?' Art said sullenly. 'I'm in enough trouble as it is.'

'That's a fine thing to say,' Joe said indignantly, 'by someone who is always preaching about the solidarity of the family.'

'I've heard enough of this,' Brad snapped. 'If you take my advice, the pair of you will go home and level with your parents. Better it comes from you first, than from elsewhere.'

'Sergant Saunders is right, Joe,' Frankie said. 'What do you think?'

'I wish to God I'd stayed back East,' Joe muttered.

'In which case you'd not have met me,' Frankie said indignantly.

Joe shook his head. 'Sorry, Frankie, it's just . . . well, it's all gotten so devilish complicated.'

'Life's never easy, Joe,' Brad said. 'It's one problem after another until the day you die. One thing is certain, you'll get nowhere if you run away — and you'll spend your life regrettin' it.'

'He's right, Joe,' Frankie said. 'Now you ride back and tell your father exactly what's happened and I'll do the same. Is that a deal?'

'OK,' Joe said, as Frankie embraced him.

'Better make it goodbye,' Art said grimly. 'Because you ain't gonna meet again, I promise you.'

* * *

'Where you been, Miss Frankie? Your pa's lookin' fer you. He's just talkin' 'bout sendin' outa search party.'

Frankie reined in Mist in front of the FC barn and dismounted.

'I'll take care of the mare, you run along and see your pa straightaway, miss.' Josh Gold, the foreman took the bridle as he spoke. There was deep concern in his eyes for he and the FC hands had worshipped the spoiled Frankie since she was a baby. He was black — as were the majority of the hands on the ranch, the result of an employment policy initiated by Frankie's grandfather which had been bitterly opposed by Raul.

Frankie ignored the concern in the man's eyes as she brushed by him without acknowledgement.

She left the barn and walked past the corral fence, conscious of several pairs of anxious eyes watching her from the bunkhouse window. For the first time in her life, the entrance to the painted timber ranch house looked forbidding rather than welcoming.

As she mounted the stoop, the door opened and the usually welcoming face of Clara, one of the servants, was apprehensive.

'Where you been, missy?' she scolded. She was a large, motherly woman, wearing a snowy white apron with a bib. The whites of her eyes shone in the gloom of the entrance as Frankie stepped inside. 'We all have been worried about you.'

'Is that you, Frankie?'

Frankie's heart sank as her father's great booming voice seemed to fill the house. Suddenly the task she had set herself seemed well-nigh insuperable.

'Your mother and father are in the study, Miss Frankie,' Clara said. 'Massa Castello ain't in a good mood. He's had us all jumpin' around like grasshoppers.'

The door opened as she approached and her father's forbidding presence filled the doorway.

'I think you've got some explaining

to do, young lady,' he said harshly.

She followed him into the room and, as he closed the door behind them, her mother, Maria, stood waiting for her, hands on hips. She was a small woman with boundless energy who had retained her lithe figure into middle age. She came from a well-to-do Mexican family and she ruled the inhabitants of the FC with her ferocious tongue.

'*Madre Mia*!' she exclaimed. 'Where you been, Frankie? Just look at the state of you.'

Frankie glanced down at herself. With a shock she saw her shirt was ripped at the neck and her pants stained with Art Castello's blood.

'Has someone been . . . interfering with you, Frankie?' her father asked, gently this time. 'If so . . . '

'I'm sorry,' Frankie said tearfully. 'But there is something dreadful I have to tell you . . . '

Her parents listened in silence as Frankie poured her heart out. She held nothing back; told them of her clandestine meetings over the last few weeks with Joe; of how the ranger had intervened at the incident at the river; and of Art Castello's admission of his involvement in the murder of his uncle and his subsequent arrest by Sergeant Saunders.

'But despite everything that's happened, I love Joe and I want to marry him,' she concluded.

'My God!' her father exclaimed. 'Had it been any other boy in the State of Texas I could have lived with it, but Raul's son — no.'

'Daddy, please . . . '

'Don't you 'Daddy' me,' her father replied furiously. 'Now go and get out of those filthy clothes and make yourself presentable for dinner.'

'I don't want any dinner,' Frankie replied as she made for the door. 'I am going to marry Joe, no matter what you say!'

As the door banged behind her daughter, Maria rounded on her husband. '*Qué pena*! You handled that very badly, Lee. Finding Dan's body must have been a dreadful shock for her. And now this. Can't you see she's on a knife edge? Do you want to drive her away forever?'

'I can do without the lecture from you,' he said, tight-lipped.

'No doubt you could, but nevertheless you are going to listen,' Maria flew back at him. 'Falling in love isn't a crime. We were in a similar position once, I believe, when our parents strongly disapproved of us. Be advised — do nothing in haste. I think that it is time you and Raul had a meeting — this feud between you has gone on far too long.'

'Meet with Raul when his son has admitted to having a part in murdering Dan? What are you thinking of?' Lee protested. 'How can we ever be reconciled now? Frankie ought to have known the trouble she would cause if she went on seeing Joe.'

'If Joe is right, then your cousin

Carlo is behind all this,' Maria said bitterly. 'I cannot understand why he favours Raul rather than you.'

Her husband's lips tightened. 'What you don't know is that Carlo is involved with the Camorra, a criminal organization which started in Naples and which is trying to establish itself over here. The Camorra's aim is nothing short of gaining complete control of everything and everyone. It does it by establishing a reign of terror. Anyone who opposes it has their face cut to ribbons or is killed. Raul has joined forces with Carlo; Dan and I refused. It seems that Dan has paid with his life.'

Maria slipped her arm inside her husband's. 'Then Carlo must be stopped before it is too late.'

Lee flung up his hands in a gesture of despair.

'What can I do?' he demanded.

'Those are not the words of a man who wishes to be elected to the state legislature,' Maria said gravely.

★ ★ ★

'Where the hell is Art?' Raul Castello demanded irritably.

Joe reined in his horse beside the corral. He dismounted and threw his bridle over the hitching post. The Bar 65 ranch was of a very similar design and layout to that of the FC, but that was only to be expected, since Raul had deliberately modelled his enterprise on the same lines as that of the inheritance he had expected from his father.

'Pa, I've got to talk with you,' Joe said. Somehow he knew he had to draw on some inner reserve he didn't know he had if he was to survive this meeting.

Raul's brow furrowed. 'Why, what's the matter, son? You ain't had bad news about your college results, have you?'

Joe warmed slightly. Despite his hard-as-nails exterior, he knew his father had a soft spot for him. Joe was everything he would have liked to have been but for the war and a dozen other things besides.

'No, it's nothing to do with that,' Joe replied. 'The results aren't posted until next week and I've no worries on that score. There's bad news, I'm afraid. I guess Ma ought to hear it, too.'

'Come on inside, boy. Stella!' Raul called out as they entered the house.

The smell of cooking filled the air and the tinkle of cutlery sounded vaguely comforting as a maid laid the dining-room table.

Stella Castello emerged from the depths of the interior. She came from a poor family who had emigrated to America from Naples and had been in the same wagon-train which brought her future husband out to Texas. She was handsome rather than beautiful, olive-skinned with black hair showing just traces of grey. Tall, full-bosomed, she was wearing a dark-red Princess polonaise dress — the current fashion. Joe stood far more in awe of his mother than his volatile father, for in the worst of crises, despite her Latin roots, his mother remained ice-cold and never lost her temper.

'So what have you got to tell us, Joe?' asked his mother.

Joe took a deep breath and launched into a full account of what had happened. He held nothing back, including his plan to marry Frankie when he qualified.

'It seems that Art has gotten himself involved with this guy, Pete Lupo,' Joe concluded. 'He's going to need a very good lawyer to get him out of this.'

His father's face took on the expression of an enraged bull.

'Don't you tell me what to do, boy, I'll be the judge of that,' he shouted. His expression became puzzled. 'When I was in town the other day, Carlo told me he believed an outlaw called Drogan was responsible for Dan's death.'

'And I don't believe any story that ranger has forced out of Art,' Stella said quietly.

'Neither do I,' Raul agreed. 'He may be a wild one but he would never stand by and see his uncle killed like that.'

Joe was thunderstruck. It was plain that nothing he said would change their minds on the subject of Art's involvement in Uncle Dan's death.

'Frankie and I want to be married,' he said quietly. 'I'd appreciate your approval.'

'My approval? To hell with that,' his father shouted. 'You knew the situation between our families. You had no right to see her behind our backs. Well, that's all finished. My only concern is getting Art out of jail. I'll go round up the boys.'

'What will you do?' his wife asked quietly. 'Take the men, ride into town and demand his release again? You are dealing with a ranger, one of a company of lawmen appointed by the state legislature — a body you are trying to join. And what if he refuses to release him again? Joe is quite right, we need a good lawyer to get Art out of this trumped-up charge.'

'He would never have got into it, if he'd stayed clear of Pete Lupo,' Joe said bitterly. 'From what I've heard that man does all Cousin Carlo's dirty work for him. It was rumoured in town that he's had a woman croupier's face slashed from ear to ear.'

'Be careful of what you are saying,' his mother said. 'Cousin Carlo is trying to help your father.'

'So that he can further his own ends,' Joe said bitterly. 'It's the Camorra, isn't it? Art told me all about it. In fact, he talks about nothing else.' He took a deep breath and held his father's lowering gaze. 'Don't you see these evil men are using you, drawing you into *la mala vita*? If you have any sense — any sense at all, you will stop all dealings with Cousin Carlo immediately.'

For a moment, Joe thought his father was going to strike him.

'Wait!' His father's fist relaxed as his wife held his arm.

'Those remarks were completely uncalled for,' Stella said to Joe. 'It is plain that you do not understand the way of the Camorra. Your brother is completely innocent, of that I am convinced. If he is in trouble, they will do their best to help him.'

Joe's eyes widened. 'You mean the Camorra will provide a lawyer?'

'But of course,' his mother replied calmly. 'The organization needs young men with brains. They will help you, too, to further your career.'

'In return for favours, no doubt,' Joe said darkly.

'And what is wrong with that?' his mother retorted. 'Only a fool refuses a helping hand when it is offered. In fact, I will go so far as to say that I do not think that your father would stand in the way of your marriage to Frankie if he could count on your support. Is that not so, Raul?'

Her husband nodded.

'I can't reconcile myself to the part Art has played in the murder of Uncle

Dan,' Joe replied, feeling his temper rising.

'Art is your brother,' his mother said.

'Are you saying I have to support him, no matter what he has done?' Joe demanded.

'You must decide whether or not your allegiance to the family is of any importance to you,' his father said. 'But I have to warn you that if it isn't, you will become an outcast.'

'And should you decide to testify against your brother, there will be a price to pay,' his mother warned. 'The arm of the Camorra is a very long one.'

Joe stared at his parents, aghast at their implacable expressions. Until now he hadn't realized just how much they were under the Camorra's influence. Were these the same people he had loved and trusted since he was a child?

'You have until after the funeral to decide,' his father said heavily.

8

Dusk was gathering outside and the lamps from the saloons and restaurants cast yellow pools of light on the boardwalk when Brad rode into town with his prisoner.

Sam Clody's jaw dropped when Brad opened the office door and locked Art Castello into a cell once more.

'He's in big trouble this time, I guess,' the old-timer remarked, when Brad finished telling him briefly what had happened. He left out the part where he had deliberately fought with Art, for he was embarrassed with himself for having been so stupid as to take another unnecessary risk.

The old-timer shot a glance at the cut on Brad's cheek with an eye as keen as a bird's. 'Looks like he didn't come without a fight,' he observed. He poured Brad a cup of coffee and handed it to him. 'You eaten yet, boy?'

When Brad shook his head, he said, 'Best you clean yourself up and go get somethin', you're gonna need all the strength you've got.'

'Why? What's happened?'

'Nothin' here. But Drogan and his men have been prowlin' the town like a pack of prairie dogs lookin' for Lupo.'

'So they must have put two and two together,' Brad mused.

'Haven't found him, though.'

'D'you reckon he's left town?'

'Not him. He's playin' hard to get. But if Drogan's lookin' for a gunfight, he'll be disappointed, that ain't the way with them Eastern varmints. I've heard those guys lurk in the dark round city blocks; they don't believe in givin' their opponents an even break. Lupo will play a waitin' game, keep Drogan guessin' — with what end in view, we'll have to wait and see.'

Brad's lips compressed. 'I could do without this. The funeral's tomorrow.'

Sam nodded and spat expertly into the spittoon. He picked up his pipe and began stuffing the bowl with tobacco. 'Be interestin' to see who comes.'

Brad stared at him. 'You don't reckon Raul Castello will be there, do you?'

'If he ain't, what are folks gonna think? Oh yes, he'll be there if he knows what's good for him — notwithstandin' you've got his boy locked up here again.'

Brad stared at the old-timer. 'Why, you've figured it all out, you crafty old so-and-so . . .'

Sam laughed. 'Listen, Brad-boy, while you go runnin' round lookin' fer trouble, someone has to do the thinkin'. At my age I guess I got precious little else to do with my time.'

Their conversation was interrupted when the door opened and Isaac Tolley, from Stranahan's Livery, rushed in. He was out of condition, unused to moving above snail's pace and stood gasping for breath almost in a state of collapse.

'What the hell's the matter, Isaac?' Sam demanded. 'You look as though you've seen a Comanche moon.'

'Thank God you're back,' Tolley said to Brad. His face was red, his forehead sheened in sweat and his breath came in short pulls. 'Jim's been killed.'

'Jim Monks?' Brad set his tin mug down with a bang and jumped to his feet. 'How?'

'I can't figure it nohow. But he's as dead as a door nail. Best you come and see for yourself.'

Brad left the old-timer in charge at the office and followed Tolley along the boardwalk until they came to the livery.

'He's out in the yard at the back.'

Tolley led the way down the aisle separating the rows of stalls and opened a door which led into a small courtyard. The liveryman struck a lucifer, lit a candle in a lantern and led Brad towards a ripening manure heap.

Brad's blood ran cold when he saw the body sprawled on the heap.

163

'Who the hell did this?' he muttered.

Tolley's nerves were so shot to pieces he couldn't speak.

Brad lifted the corpse off the heap and inspected it under the light of the lantern. Ostensibly there was no sign of how death had occurred.

'Here, hold it steady,' he snapped at Tolley.

It was an impossible demand, for he could hear the liveryman's teeth chattering as he carefully inspected the back of the head of the corpse. Despite the swaying lantern, he knew what he was looking for — and it was there, the hole in the mouth.

Jim Monks had been executed in the same way as Dan Castello!

As Brad rose to his feet, the anger of the waste of such a decent young life rose inside him.

Isaac Tolley found his voice at last. 'Jim was on duty this evening. I went home for something to eat. When I came back, he was nowhere around. It was ages before I found him.'

Brad's jaw hardened. Lupo must have seen him bringing in Art Castello. Lupo must have figured he had spoken to the liveryman and put two and two together . . . and now Jim Monks was dead, one of his key witnesses was silenced forever.

Suddenly he bethought himself: if Jim Monks had been murdered to keep his mouth shut, Art Castello must also be in danger.

And so must Sam Clody.

'I gotta get back to the office,' Brad told Isaac Tolley. Gun in hand, he darted through the door of the livery stable, letting the door bang behind him. His face creased with anxiety, he ran with giant strides along the boardwalk back to the office.

He needn't have worried, for Sam had closed the battle shutters and it was some time before the old-timer had all the bolts drawn, opened the door, and stood facing him Winchester in hand, a quizzical look on his gnarled features.

'Sam, thank God you're OK.' Brad sighed with relief as he collapsed into a chair. 'Jim Monks has been murdered. Lupo must have figured it was him who put me on to his meeting with Art Castello. I should never have brought Art Castello back here, I ought to have figured Lupo and his boys might try to pull somethin'.'

'You ain't thinkin' straight, Brad-boy, and that's a fact,' Sam said. 'What do you take me, for? I ain't gonna play the sittin' duck, invitin' trouble. When the odds are stacked against you, you gotta stay one step ahead. I wouldn't have survived this long without I learned that.'

Brad winced at the old-timer's stinging rebuke. But even as he spoke so he thought of Renate and the terrified woman she was looking after . . .

★ ★ ★

Sam let Brad out by the back way into an alley as black as a canyon on

166

a moonless night.

'Now mind how you go, son,' he said, before he closed the door. 'Don't let your anxiety for them women get in the way of your own survival, you're no use to 'em iffen your dead.'

Taking his advice to heart, Brad avoided the main thoroughfare, door-hopping between the premises through quiet side streets, gun at the ready, every sense alert, ready to shoot the head off a rat if one showed itself. But apart from a cat taking sudden flight and knocking over a pail with a tremendous clatter, the way was clear — but as a precaution he approached Renate's house from the rear.

It took three or four stones rattling against the shutter, before it opened and she looked down at him.

'*Mamma mia*! Who is it? What on earth do you want at this time of night?'

'It's Brad Saunders. Let me in and I'll explain.'

He waited, vigilant, until she unbolted

the door and he stepped inside and closed it behind him without delay.

Her hair was down, she was barefoot and she was wearing a dressing-gown over her nightdress. She led him through to the parlour. Her raw-boned features were silhouetted in the light of the lamp she lit.

'This had better be good,' she said, a hint of primness in her voice. 'I have a reputation to protect.'

'I'm sorry to disturb you so late, but I had to come and warn you,' he said holstering the gun.

'About what?'

'First of all, Beulah — is she OK?'

When Renate nodded, he asked, 'Has she told you who did that to her?'

'I have already told you — it was the Camorra.'

'But why?'

'Drogan persuaded her to leave a side-door unlocked so that he could rob Manzoni.' Renate smiled ironically.

Brad stared at her.

'I didn't believe it at first.'

168

'So Manzoni must have found out that Beulah had helped Drogan. Did he cut her face?'

Renate shook her head. 'Manzoni is the *capo*. He doesn't do that kind of thing.' She shivered. 'Pete Lupo does the dirty work. That man makes my flesh creep.'

'Isn't Beulah still in great danger, then?'

'Only if she talks — and she won't do that. Not if she knows what's good for her. She'll never go into a witness stand, if that is what you're hoping. The scar will be a permanent reminder to her.'

Brad felt his blood run cold. In the big cities back East, it took an entire police force to fight gangs of criminals such as this. What could he and one old-timer expect to achieve? It was no use telegraphing Captain Hall for help for as yet he didn't have a single witness to testify against the Camorra.

He took no satisfaction in the fact that he and Sam were reduced to the status of spectators on the side-lines of a battle between two ruthless men backed by teams of hardened killers. There must be something he could do to prevent himself and Sam from being caught up in a sequence of events over which they had no control whatsoever.

Brad rose to leave and Renate accompanied him to the door.

'It's Dan's funeral tomorrow,' she said. 'I just hope we can give him a decent burial.'

Brad sensed the disquiet in her voice. 'Do you think Raul will come?' he enquired.

Renate's eyebrows raised. 'But of course. What would people think if he didn't? We are family, after all.'

Brad pondered for a moment. Then he said, 'Somethin' about this whole business don't ring true. I can't believe that Carlo Manzoni has your brother murdered simply to help Raul become a member of the state legislature. There has to be more to it than that.'

Renate was silent for a moment.

Then she said, 'You are a very persistent man, Brad.'

'It's my job,' he replied. 'I ain't quittin' until I get to the bottom of this business.'

She sighed. 'I suppose you ought to know, for you will find out sooner or later.'

'Well?'

'Dan was a good man, but he wasn't perfect.'

Brad could see she was having difficulty in coming to terms with what she was about to reveal, but he kept discreetly silent.

'My brother never married, but all his life he found solace in a certain kind of woman. Not soiled doves — he was too fastidious for those, you understand?'

Brad nodded. He recalled Marie Madelaine, a beautiful singer, a former Civil War spy and courier for counterfeit currency who had all but twisted him round her little finger . . . but that was another story.

'Dan thought I didn't know, of

course. He was very discreet about it.'

'Who is . . . ' Brad corrected himself. '*Was* it?'

Renate hesitated. 'Can't you guess?'

Brad took a deep breath. 'Not Beulah!' he exclaimed. 'Renate, I'm real sorry I brought her here. If I'd had the slightest idea . . . '

'Please don't apologize.'

Brad thought for a moment. Then, on impulse, he asked, 'Was Carlo Manzoni involved with her, too?'

Renate nodded. 'She hated Manzoni, the way he took over the saloon and expected to have her as well. When she heard the news that Dan was dead, she suspected Manzoni was behind it. That was why she co-operated with Drogan. She wanted to get back at Manzoni.'

'Revenge?'

'Back in Italy, we call it *vendetta*,' Renate said.

'In view of what you've just told me,' Brad observed. 'I am surprised you want to keep Beulah under your roof.'

Renate smiled. 'I think that she has learned a very hard lesson. She has spoken with Father O'Brien. She has made her confession. She wishes to put her past behind her and start afresh.'

'After what she has done?' Brad said, scarcely containing the cynicism in his voice.

'No life is beyond redemption, Brad,' Renate said quietly. She stood on tiptoe and kissed him gently. For a moment he was tempted to make a positive response, but now was not the time.

'Take care, won't you?' she said, as she closed the door behind him.

As Brad emerged from the house, the sound of firing came from the centre of town. Abandoning his previous caution, he drew his gun and ran along the street until he came to the main thoroughfare where, despite the lateness of the hour, he saw a large crowd of people were gathering around the entrance to the Lucky Black Cat Saloon . . .

'I'm tired of lookin' for these guys,' Falcon said. 'If you ask me, they ran like rabbits once they heard we were on to them.'

He was standing with Butch Lord at the bar of the Lucky Black Cat Saloon. Both men were smoking and drinking beer.

'Where's the boss?' Lord asked. He glanced at the clock. 'He said to meet him here at nine o'clock sharp.'

'Here he comes, now,' Falcon said.

The batwings opened and Drogan beckoned to the two men. They downed their glasses and did his bidding.

'Any luck, boss?' Lord asked, when they were out on the sidewalk.

Gross appeared out of the shadows and the men coalesced into a tight group in the pale-yellow light from the saloon windows.

'You've found nothing, I take it?' Drogan asked Falcon and Lord as they left the sidewalk and turned down an alley.

When both men shook their heads, he said, 'Well, I guess we done gone all day with never a sign of any of 'em. It's as though they've disappeared off the face of the earth . . .'

Drogan's voice tailed off as a group of three men emerged from the darkness and came to a halt in front of them.

'No need for you to look any more, Drogan,' a voice said. 'We're here.'

'Why, Lupo . . .'

The first bullet cut Drogan down, the precursor of a fusillade of shots which in the narrow alley seemed to merge into a solid wall of sound. A hail of bullets swept the alley, every one hitting their mark, riddling their targets.

It was all over in seconds. By the time the first curious heads peered tentatively through the batwings of the Lucky Black Cat, the alley was empty except for four corpses lying in an ever-widening pool of blood . . .

175

★ ★ ★

Brad shouldered his way through the crowd and came upon the sight of four men, sprawled in various attitudes in the alley. With the help of one of the more sanguine bystanders, he dragged them one by one onto the boardwalk. From the light through the saloon windows, he saw it was Drogan and his men. It was murder, that was plain to see, each corpse had been riddled with heavy-calibre bullets and not one of them had managed to draw his gun.

'Did anyone see who did this?'

Brad's question was purely rhetorical, for he knew what the answer would be. But in his own mind he hadn't the slightest doubt that this was the work of Lupo and his men.

'See it? Not on your life. Christ, man, I thought a reg'ment was firing,' a tall, thin man with a cadaverous face said. 'I thought it was never gonna stop.'

Brad set about the task of organizing the removal of the bodies to Dr Maguire's mortuary. He and Zack Trimble, the local carpenter who specialized in making furniture and coffins, received no further help from the onlookers, most of whom seemed to be in a state of shock.

'My word, Zack, we are busy,' Dr Maguire said, when the buckboard drew up outside his house. He approached them, holding a lantern.

'We're doin' a roaring trade,' the carpenter agreed.

'Six autopsies in two days is surely going some,' Dr Maguire agreed. 'There'll be more dead than alive in this town before we're through.'

For some reason, Trimble thought the remark funny. He had an infectious laugh to which Brad was immune, but it caught the doctor, and the two men only stopped when the doctor's wife flung open a window and berated the pair of them for waking the children.

Brad said nothing. Maybe doctors

and undertakers had to be light-hearted about death to keep their sanity. He had seen enough on the battlefield; he figured he ought to be used to it, but somehow he knew he could never be remotely cheerful in the presence of it.

'By the way, Sergeant Saunders, I can confirm your suspicion that Jim Monks was killed by the same method as used on Dan Castello,' Maguire said in a loud whisper, when they had carried the corpses inside. 'And as for these, well, I don't think you need me to tell you the cause of death. It's lead poisoning, as you call it out here. On a grand scale.' He looked closely at Drogan's body. 'And they weren't using pop-guns this time. In fact I would go as far as to say that this is a clear case of overkill.'

9

The following day dawned clear and bright in contrast to the heavy stormcloud of fear which hung over Roberta.

'I reckon Lupo's made his play,' Brad said to Sam, as he sipped his coffee. 'So where do we go from here?'

Sam finished his daily inspection of his Winchester and laid it aside. 'We need feel no conscience about what happened to Drogan and his boys, they got what was comin' to 'em. Lupo has saved us a whole heap of trouble. My guess is he will lie low 'til after the funeral. What we gotta look out for now is a confrontation between Raul and Lee Castello.'

Brad glanced at Sam. He may be old, but his brain was functioning and his reading of the situation was razor-sharp.

179

'What about Manzoni?' he mused.

Sam lit his pipe and puffed out a cloud of tobacco. 'He'll be there, of course. As mayor of this town, it's his duty. And as far as I know, you've got nothin' on him.'

Which was perfectly true. He was convinced that Carlo Manzoni was the spider at the centre of this web, but there was nothing to link him with anything that had happened.

'I got nothing on Lupo, either.'

Which was true. There had been no witnesses to the massacre in the alley outside the Lucky Black Cat and no witness to the murder of Jim Monks. Beulah would be too terrified to testify. There was only Art Castello who had foolishly admitted to the part he had played in the murder of his uncle and would retract it as soon as he entered a court of law.

'He's the joker in the pack,' Sam said, thumbing over his shoulder at the cells where Castello sat munching stolidly through his breakfast. 'What's his pa gonna do about him this time?'

'Get him a good lawyer, I guess,' Brad replied. 'No doubt he'll get him out on bail.'

'In that case he'd better watch his back,' the oldtimer said.

* * *

There was little sign of activity in the town as the next three hours dragged by. The numbing effect of the previous night's massacre together with unease at the impending funeral combined to make even the most sanguine of citizens fearful of what might happen next.

Brad judged it prudent to remain indoors with Sam, smoking and drinking coffee until half an hour before noon. The sound of approaching horsemen brought him to his feet.

'Here comes Lee Castello and his family,' Sam said, as he opened the door and squinted into the blinding sunshine.

Brad stepped outside just as Lee Castello pulled up the buckboard carrying himself, Frankie and an elegant woman he correctly surmised was Lee's wife. The entire family were dressed in mourning clothes.

'Good morning, Sergeant Saunders,' Lee said. 'This is Maria, my wife. You know Frankie, of course.'

'Didn't you bring some of your men along with you?' Brad asked him, as the group assembled in the office, still darkened by the drawn-down battle shutters.

'Why no,' Lee said. 'I heard you had banned weapons worn within the town limits — a policy I entirely endorse, by the way. In the event I judged that the presence of a large body of my men either inside or outside town might be provocative. To be honest, Sergeant Saunders, despite many misgivings, I personally have never given up hope of a reconciliation with Raul.'

Frankie grimaced her amazement. Brad nodded. It was the first ray of

182

hope to pierce the heavy cloud of pessimism that had hung over him ever since he had found Dan Castello's body in the Neuces.

'Frankie tells me you've arrested Raul's son again,' Lee said. 'If he's played a part in Dan's death, that's terrible news.'

'Sergeant Saunders, I must say I am appalled at this turn of events,' Maria Castello said. 'When the news breaks it will do untold damage to our family.'

'It's worse than you imagine,' Brad replied. Lee Castello and his family listened in stunned silence as he recounted the events of the previous night.

'I still can't believe Raul is involved with these people,' Lee said, when Brad had finished. 'Dan made it quite clear that the Camorra are bad news and events are proving him right.'

'Your brother's on the way now,' Sam reported from the door.

Brad waited while Raul came into the office. He was accompanied by his wife and son, Joe. Raul stopped dead when he saw his brother and his heavy eyelids narrowed. For a few moments Brad was conscious of the antipathy between the two men forking the air like lightning in a dry storm.

'We've got trouble enough, Raul,' Lee said suddenly in a choked voice. 'Dan's dead. How about we call a truce until after the funeral?'

His brother gave an almost imperceptible nod. He turned to Brad. 'Meantime, I'd like another word with my boy.'

Brad led Raul Castello to the cell. As he opened it, he said, 'He's in big trouble this time. He's confessed to having a part in the murder of your brother.'

'Whatever he's been sayin', it's all lies, Pa,' Art Castello said furiously. 'Saunders had it in for me since the day he first set eyes on me.'

'Don't worry, son, I'll get you out of this,' his father said. 'Just wait until after the funeral.'

When Raul Castello saw his son's bruised and battered face, he rounded on Brad. 'Seems to me like you beat the confession out of him. If that's the way you Rangers operate, it's high time the force was disbanded.'

★ ★ ★

As Sam Clody, rifle in hand, watched the funeral party, accompanied by Brad, leave the sheriff's office, he gave a sigh of relief. However, with that crisis over, it left the way clear for the next and the ex-ranger having led a life steeped in unfortuate happenings, fell to pondering where the next one would spring from.

Dust swirled along the empty street outside. The bell was tolling from the tower of the Catholic church. Most of the townsfolk were attending the funeral, for Dan Castello had been a highly respected figure in the community.

With the door locked, the battle

shutters down and the prisoner slumped quietly in his cell, Sam laid his rifle on his desk and reached for his pipe. He stuffed it with tobacco, lit it and puffed contentedly all the while reflecting on the strange things which motivated mankind. All his life Sam Clody had been a keen student of the ways of his fellow man and, profiting from experience, had become a man wise in the ways of the world.

It was hot and airless in the enclosed office and he was drowsily drifting in a sea of remembrance when the tap came on the door.

A lifetime of caution brought him instantly alert. He laid aside his cold pipe and grabbed his Winchester.

The knock came again. It was insistent, yet gentle.

A woman's knock?

He walked over to the door.

'Who's there?' he asked through the woodwork.

'It's me, Beulah.'

Her voice sounded strangely muffled.

'Wait,' Sam said.

He laid his rifle aside and half-opened one of the battle shutters. Beulah was standing alone on the boardwalk. Her once-beautiful face was still swathed in bandages.

Sam checked out again. Satisfied she was on her own, he closed the battle shutter and walked over to the door. It was secured by a lock, bolts and, as a final precaution, a heavy chain which permitted it to be opened slightly.

'Please let me in,' Beulah begged, as Sam peered through the gap. Her voice was indistinct for the movement of her jaw was severely restricted by the bandages. 'My life is in danger.'

Without further ado, Sam unhooked the chain and stood aside to allow the woman to enter. She had hardly crossed the threshold when she was propelled inside by a push which sent her staggering. Sam made a vain snatch for his rifle but the passing years had slowed him down and Pete Lupo got there before him. He was accompanied by two men Sam recognized as his *compadres*. They were all armed with snub-nosed derringers.

'What the hell is going on?' Sam demanded. He stared at Beulah, furious at first at her apparent betrayal, but from the terror in her eyes he divined she was acting under duress.

'Stand aside, old man, if you want to live to a ripe old age,' Lupo said with a sneer.

From inside the cell there came a whoop of delight from Art Castello as he figured out what was happening.

'The keys.' Lupo held out his hand to Sam as imperiously as a Roman emperor.

With a heavy heart, Sam shambled over to the desk, took them out of a drawer and passed them to him.

'Keep an eye on him,' Lupo ordered Cerioli. 'Watch the street,' he ordered Rocca.

Lupo picked up Sam's beloved Winchester and ejected the shells. He tossed it into a corner before striding along the short corridor which led to the cells.

Better keep my mouth shut, Sam told himself. These guys are pure poison.

There was a clanking noise as Lupo opened the cell door.

'Thanks, Pete, I knew you wouldn't let me down,' Art Castello cried jubilantly. Suddenly his tone of voice changed to one of alarm. 'Say, what is this?'

Sam froze as he heard the short bark of the derringer. There was the noise of a heavily falling body and then silence until Lupo emerged, the barrel of the derringer still smoking.

'OK, old man.'

As he grabbed Sam roughly by the arm and propelled him towards the cell, the old-timer figured his time had come. Inside the cell, Art Castello's body lay sprawled on the floor. He was dead. Sam had seen too many corpses not to know that.

For the first time in his life, Sam felt the terrible apprehension of death felt by the old when they feel powerless to help themselves. Lupo stood before him, pointing his derringer at him, a man whom Sam, in the prime of life, would have challenged and defeated, but now he knew that although inside he was still eighteen, his body would no longer follow his spirit's urgent commands.

'I will not kill you,' Lupo said tonelessly. 'For when he returns, I require you to tell Sergeant Saunders that I am waiting for him at the Lucky Black Cat Saloon.'

The door slammed shut, the key turned.

'Bring her!'

The woman gave a muffled cry of fear as Lupo uttered the command to his men.

And then Sam was left alone in the cell with the sightless eyes of Art Castello staring at him.

He had been shot through the mouth.

* * *

'*Requiescat in pace.*'

The priest's last words were spoken. The funeral was over. Dan Castello's body was interred. The crowd of citizens who had attended began to disperse conversing in low respectful tones. The men were wearing black suits and ties, the womenfolk black dresses and black silk headscarves.

Standing beside the two bare-headed gravediggers in the hot sunshine, Brad kept a respectful distance maintaining a watchful eye on the proceedings while, after the formality of the requiem mass and interment, the black-cassocked Father O'Brien spoke a few words of condolence to the briefly united Castello family.

Renate Castello caught Brad's eye and gave him an enigmatic smile. How such an attractive woman had kept her resolve to remain single knowing of her brother's liaisons was something he would never understand.

Carlo Manzoni was there too, he noticed. Smooth, suave, not quite smiling, he played the discreet, grieving relative to perfection. When the priest had finished the ceremony and shaken hands, the party walked slowly towards the cemetery gates.

Brad quickened his pace to catch Manzoni.

'I'd like a word with you,' Brad said in low voice.

'Not now, Sergeant, the time is hardly appropriate,' Manzoni replied.

'For what I've got to ask, I guess it never will be,' Brad replied. 'I want to know where I can find Pete Lupo.'

Manzoni's eyebrows raised. He took out a silver cigar case, opened it, and then, mindful of the fact that he was still inside the precincts of the cemetery, replaced it.

'I am afraid I can't help you there,' he said.

'You surprise me,' Brad said. 'It's common knowledge that he works for you.'

The name of Lupo had attracted Raul Castello's attention. He left the others to join Brad and Manzoni.

'You told me the other day that the outlaw Drogan killed Dan,' he said to Manzoni accusingly.

'I believed that to be the case,' his cousin replied.

'Trouble is, we can't check it out, seeing that Drogan and his gang will be buried here later today.'

'That's a great pity,' Manzoni agreed.

'Problem is this ranger says my son Art has admitted to kidnapping Dan who was then shot by Pete Lupo. What have you to say to that?'

Manzoni flicked a hair off the lapel of his immaculately tailored suit and shrugged his shoulders.

'Of that and Mr Lupo's whereabouts I know nothing.'

Manzoni returned the hard stares of both Brad and his cousin with a pose of studied equanimity which would have done credit to an actor.

'It seems to me that your son is going

to need a good lawyer,' Manzoni said smoothly. 'That is no problem. It will take a little time, of course, for I must contact my people in New York. In the meantime, I am sure we can arrange for bail. Would you like me to proceed?'

'I guess so,' Raul said resignedly.

As Brad left the cemetery, Frankie, accompanied by Joe, came across to him.

'We both told our parents, like you said,' Frankie told him.

'And?'

'Mine don't like it, but I guess they'll come round,' Frankie said.

'I don't think so,' Joe said. 'Despite what happened, they don't accept that Art had anything to do with Uncle Dan's murder. They say they will cut me off if I testify against him. They are dropping strong hints that the Camorra will take revenge if I do.'

'What can we do?' Frankie asked Brad.

'Nothing for the moment,' Brad replied. 'You've got time on your side.

In the meantime, I've got to find Pete Lupo.'

He left the young couple standing forlornly by the cemetery gates, and walked the short distance back into town. Roberta was coming back to life again now the funeral was over; it was surprising how quickly the crowds dispersed, the shutters were raised and business resumed as usual.

He walked up the steps onto the boardwalk and paused before the door, puzzled. The battle shutters were down, but the door was open, the hinges creaking as it swung gently in the warm breeze.

He drew his gun, cocked it and pushed the door open with his foot, following it inside in a gunfighter's crouch.

The outer office was empty. Sam's rifle lay discarded on the floor amongst a pile of discarded shells.

'That you, Brad-boy?'

Brad heaved a sigh of relief at the sound of the old-timer's voice. He moved along the short corridor and stopped dead when he saw that Sam was locked inside the cell with Art Castello's corpse.

'What the hell happened?' he demanded of Sam.

Sam was so overcome with emotion, it took him a few moments before he could speak.

'There's a spare set of keys in the bottom drawer, Brad,' he said at last. 'For God's sake get me outa here.'

Brad hastened to comply with his request. While Sam went through to the outer office he quickly inspected the corpse.

Art Castello had been shot through the mouth.

When Brad went back into the outer office, the old-timer said, 'Give me a shot of whiskey to steady my nerves and I'll tell you what happened.'

Sam recovered his rifle and reloaded it as he recounted his story.

'I figured Beulah had duped me at first,' he concluded. 'But that ain't the case. Lupo and his men were right behind her. The poor woman was afeared out of her wits.'

'And now Lupo is holding her hostage at the Lucky Black Cat Saloon,' Brad said.

He took out his gun and checked it.

As he strode towards the door, Sam said, 'Where you goin', boy?'

'Where do you think?' Brad replied. 'It's time this business was ended once and for all.'

Sam rose to his feet. 'One thing's certain, Bradboy, you ain't goin' alone.'

'Sam, you've had a nasty shock. You'd best rest up and stay outa this.'

The old-timer's lips curled in a fierce snarl.

'I ain't through yet. You just try and stop me. I gotta score to settle with Pete Lupo.'

10

As Brad emerged from the sheriff's office, he ran into Renate Castello who was hurrying along the boardwalk.

'Brad, I've just been back home. Dan's office has been broken into and a lot of his files have been stolen. And Beulah isn't there,' she said.

Brad's lips tightened. 'Manzoni is a very thorough man. My guess is that Lupo has taken Beulah hostage.'

'*Dio mio*!' she exclaimed. 'I left her just while I attended the funeral. Why has he taken her?'

'He used her to gain entrance here. He's murdered Raul's son.'

Renate was stunned.

'Art had admitted to me that he had a hand in your brother's death,' Brad said. 'He set up his uncle and Lupo shot him.'

'Art was involved? I don't believe

it. Even I did not know what the Camorra are truly capable of,' Renate said brokenly.

'Not for any longer, miss,' Sam said. 'We're goin' to the Lucky Black Cat to smoke 'em out.'

'What?' Renate stared at Brad. 'How can you and this old man possibly arrest a man like Lupo?'

Sam drew himself up to his full height. He had pinned on his old ranger badge and polished it until it gleamed and winked in the bright sunlight. 'Beggin' your pardon, young woman. I was in the ranger service before you was born. I've fought Indians, Mexicans and arrested outlaws by the score. I've never run scared from any man in my life and I don't plan on starting now.'

'I'm sorry,' Renate said. 'It is just that I care too much about you both to see you die at the hands of that *camorristi* scum.' She turned to Brad, fighting back the tears welling in her eyes. 'If you must go, don't go on your own. Not just the two of you.'

'So who do you suggest goes with us?' asked Brad. 'This whole town's runnin' scared.'

'Let me go and speak with Lee and Raul,' Renate replied.

'Can't see what good that'll do,' Brad said. 'It's plain those two will never see eye to eye.'

'Let me give it a try. Please. Raul may change his mind when he hears what has happened to his son,' Renate begged.

Brad caught the old-timer's eyes and nodded.

'OK. Ten minutes and we're movin' out.'

After Renate had left, the two men withdrew inside the office. Brad rolled a smoke and Sam lit his pipe. They smoked in silence until Brad glanced at the clock on the wall and said, 'Time's up, I guess.'

He was in the process of grinding out his cigarette butt in the ashtray when the door burst open and Raul Castello, followed by his brother Lee, strode into the office.

'Renate just told me what Lupo did to my son,' Raul said his voice thick with emotion. 'Is it true?'

'As God is my witness,' Sam said. 'His body is still lying there in the cell.'

'I am prepared to help you,' Lee said to Brad, as his brother hurried through to the cell. 'But I cannot speak for him.'

Raul returned a few moments later, his face contorted with rage and grief.

'I guess I'm through with Manzoni and his *camorristi*,' he said. 'Count me in.'

'Thank God you have seen the light,' Renate said fervently, 'before it is too late.'

'Now wait a minute,' Brad said. 'You are two respectable citizens, up for election to the state legislature. Flushin' Lupo and his men outa that bear hole of a saloon ain't gonna be easy. Manzoni is playin' for high stakes. You gotta remember that if

Lupo defeats us, the Camorra will seize power in this area.'

'From what I've heard of your Captain Hall, that state of affairs wouldn't last for very long,' Lee said.

'Manzoni doesn't think that way,' Brad said. 'He figures that even a man like Captain Hall has his price.'

'Must you confront Lupo?' asked Renate. 'Why not send for more rangers?'

'I'm not waiting around any longer,' Raul said. 'Give us some weapons and let's go get those guys.'

'Wait!' Brad said, as the brothers headed for the door. 'Now you just listen. We can't go charging in without a plan. I'm responsible for what happens and I say how we handle this, is that clear?' He paused to let it sink in, before he said to the brothers, 'Now with respect, just what fightin' experience do you two gentlemen have?'

'We both served in the war for the duration,' Lee informed him.

'I was wounded in Pickett's charge on Cemetery Ridge,' Raul said.

'And I was wounded in the Union Army defending it,' Lee added quietly.

'Gettysburg!' Sam exclaimed. 'Sergeant Saunders and I were both there with Jeb Stuart's cavalry. Too many good men died that day.' He wiped a little tear from his eye. 'I guess I'm gettin' old and emotional.' He looked at Raul and held out his hand. 'No hard feelin's, huh?'

'Never thought I'd ever shake hands with a Johnny Reb,' Raul said, as the two men's hands met.

'Quit the reminiscin', you'll have us all blubberin',' Brad said, as he went over to the gun racks. He took down two Winchester rifles and threw one to each of the brothers.

'So we all know what fighting's about,' he announced, as the two men checked and loaded their weapons. 'And if you will all do as I say, the Camorra's gonna learn, too.'

★ ★ ★

In the confines of the Lucky Black Cat Saloon, Luca Cerioli and Umberto Rocca were getting restless. The saloon had been cleared of both staff and customers. Rumour had travelled rapidly and the citizens of Roberta, in going about their daily business, were very wisely leaving the vicinity of the saloon well alone. They were standing where Lupo had stationed them at the top of the staircase — a strategic spot from which they could command the batwing doors.

'When Saunders appears, wipe him out,' was Lupo's parting instruction.

'Where the hell is he?' Cerioli said.

'I reckon he's chickened out,' Rocca said. 'I never rated that guy at all. These Western lawmen can't hold a candle to a New York cop.'

Cerioli sniggered. 'Their outlaws are no better. Drogan and his men were just a bunch of pussycats. Parading round town, flaunting their weapons.

Fancy letting themselves get trapped like that.'

Both men checked the mechanisms of their Evans guns for the umpteenth time.

'I don't understand why the *capo* ordered Lupo to kill Castello's son,' Cerioli said. 'I thought they were family.'

'The boy must have said something,' Rocca said. 'Otherwise why would the ranger have arrested him again?'

'Raul Castello is learning the hard way. He had better toe the line, otherwise he's a dead man.' Cerioli grinned. 'Coming out West has proved to be quite something, hasn't it? And there was me thinking it would be a waste of time.'

'Wait!' His companion gripped his arm. 'There's someone coming along the boardwalk.'

The footsteps stopped outside the batwings and a voice called out, 'It's Raul Castello.'

'Do you reckon it's a trap?' Cerioli

glanced at Rocca as he spoke.

'Only one way to find out,' Rocca replied.

'OK, Castello. Open the batwings and come inside with your hands held high,' Cerioli called. 'If anyone else is with you, you are a dead man.'

'I'm supposed to be on your side,' Raul said, as he pushed open the batwings and stepped inside the saloon. 'Where's the boss? I've got some important information for him.'

Cerioli and Rocca lowered their weapons when they saw Raul was unarmed.

And that was their undoing, for behind him the batwings crashed open. Raul hit the deck and Lee Castello and Sam Clody entered the saloon their rifles at the ready.

'Drop them weapons, you're under arrest,' Sam Clody ordered.

'You must be joking,' Cerioli said with a sneer.

Before his gun barrel could reach horizontal, Sam was squeezing the trigger on his Winchester. Lee did the same and the noise of the two weapons firing merged into a roar of sound as they pumped a barrage of lead into the two *camorristi*.

★ ★ ★

Brad was waiting, gun in hand, outside the side door of the saloon in the alley. He smiled grimly as the firing began, neither Sam nor Lee were in a mood to take prisoners. After an initial challenge, they were carrying out his orders to the letter.

The sound of the door lock being shot away was lost in the sound of gunfire and a few moments later, Brad was pounding up the wooden staircase, two steps at a time. A glance showed him the rooms at the top were empty and, as he burst out onto the upper floor, he came face to face with Lupo.

Even as Brad brought his gun to bear, he choked back for he saw Lupo was holding Beulah. Lupo was holding a derringer and with a smile of triumph at Brad's indecision, he took aim . . .

* * *

Down below in the saloon, Sam's experience told him to maintain his vigilance. Whilst Lee Castello was helping his brother back to his feet, Sam's eyes swept the saloon and came to rest on Beulah who was peering down at him from the top of the staircase. Behind her was the shadowy figure of a man he knew could only be Lupo.

Where the hell was Brad?

Suddenly the sound of pounding feet from upstairs drew Lupo's attention. From the bottom of the staircase, Sam raised his rifle as he saw Lupo's attention distracted. As he raised his rifle and took aim, for a few seconds Lupo's back was exposed as he whirled round keeping Beulah in front of him to face the threat from his rear.

It was a difficult shot and with hindsight Sam was the first to admit he could have easily missed. The bullet grazed across Lupo's right shoulder-blade, scoring a bloody path across the back of his neck.

'Half an inch lower and he'd have been a dead man,' Sam was wont to say when recounting the tale afterwards.

Lupo released Beulah who stumbled and fell, screaming in fear as she fell off the top step. Lee and Raul saw it and dashed forward to catch her as she rolled over and over down the carpeted stairs.

Lupo made a dash for the corridor which lay beyond with Brad in pursuit.

Brad was ice cool now, his main worries were over for two of the *camorristi* were dead and everyone else, including the woman, were in one piece, even if somewhat knocked about. As far as he was concerned it was himself versus Lupo, man on man, the way he had always wanted it.

But now was not the time to lose vigilance. The man who was disappearing round the far end of the corridor was as cunning as the animal which gave him his name.

The truth of this was exemplified when Lupo paused and fired a volley of shots back at Brad, forcing him to flatten himself against the wall, praying he wouldn't be hit by a richochet.

As Brad resumed the chase he saw his quarry was wounded, for a trail of blood spattered the uncarpeted corridor which ran past the wooden partitioned rooms which formed the brothel.

Reaching the end of the corridor, Brad realized Lupo had entered one of these rooms. Pausing to check his weapon, he kicked the door open. The room was empty, the bed in disarray. The window was open, a trail of blood led to it and, when Brad looked outside, he saw that Lupo had climbed through it and had taken to the rooftop.

The roof of the saloon was flat, as was the next building on the other side of the alley and Brad ran after Lupo, amazed at the man's agility, despite the fact he must be losing a lot of blood.

The gap across the alley loomed in front of Lupo and he paused, obviously assessing his chances of making the leap across it.

Seeing Lupo's dilemma, Brad stopped and called out, 'Give yourself up, you don't have a chance of making that jump.'

Lupo looked round desperately. The expression on his face was like a cornered animal.

'You aren't going to take me, Ranger,' he snarled.

In the chase, Brad saw Lupo had dropped his gun. Arresting him now seemed a foregone conclusion. But Lupo had other ideas. As Brad approached, he turned and made the attempt to leap the gap across to the next building. He almost made it, his hands scrabbled at the woodwork, but weakened by the loss of blood, he was unable to hold on and he fell into the alley below.

'Looks like he done broke his neck,'

Sam said laconically when Brad joined the old-timer and the brothers in the centre of the crowd of people thronging the alley.

'The power of the Camorra in Castello County is broken,' Lee said.

He looked at his brother and as their eyes met, they smiled and their hands met in a firm clasp.

'Lee, I want you to know I'm withdrawing my candidature for the state legislature,' Raul said. 'You're the best man for the job and I'll support you all the way.'

Lee smiled. 'If we join forces who can defeat us? We're back as a family, I guess.'

'Is Beulah OK?' Brad enquired.

'Renate is taking care of her,' Lee said. 'She's had a nasty fall, but she'll be fine.'

'Where's Manzoni?' Brad asked suddenly.

'We'd better check out the hotel,' Lee said.

Accompanied by the two brothers,

Brad hurried across the street.

'I'm sorry, Sergeant Saunders, but Mr Manzoni left for the station ten minutes ago,' the lobby clerk informed them. 'He said he had urgent business in New York.'

'I bet he has,' Brad said grimly.

'The train leaves at four o'clock,' Lee said. 'If we hurry, we just might catch him.'

'It's worth a try,' Raul urged.

'Come on then,' Brad said.

The three men raced with giant strides along the street towards the station.

Manzoni was standing beside the track, holding a small suitcase. The siren of the approaching engine announced its arrival.

'Let me handle this,' Raul said to Brad as the train clanked to a grinding halt in a cloud of steam.

'Carlo!' Raul called out, as his cousin made to mount the step up to the carriage. 'I want a word with you.'

'Not now,' Manzoni replied irritably.

'Can't you see I'm catching this train!'

'Not now, you aren't,' Raul said. He interposed himself roughly between his cousin and the train, forcing him to drop his suitcase. 'I guess you've got some explaining to do.'

'I must ask you to get on board, gentlemen,' the conductor said. 'We're leaving right away.'

'Get out of my way,' Manzoni snarled.

'You're staying here,' Raul shouted.

As he grabbed his cousin by the collar of his jacket, Manzoni's hand flashed inside it and withdrew a derringer.

'No!' Lee shouted in desperation for his brother.

In front of horrified faces of the passengers, Brad's Colt cleared leather in a fluid movement.

'Drop it, Manzoni.' His voice cut through the noise of hissing steam from the locomotive.

Manzoni whirled round and, as he did so, Brad knew from a wealth of experience that he intended to fire.

Both weapons discharged simultaneously at a distance of less than ten feet. Brad felt a numbing blow to his right shoulder and stumbled forward, conscious of his own weapon bucking in his hand as he did so.

* * *

When he came to, he was lying in a clean bed the sheets of which smelt of lavender. Apart from a dull, burning sensation in his right shoulder, he felt OK. His eyes came to focus on a crucifix facing him on the wall. A bunch of freshly picked flowers was arranged in a vase beneath it.

There was a rustle and Renate bent over him. She smiled when she saw he was awake.

'Dr Maguire said you'd be all right,' she said. 'If you do as he says and rest up awhile, you'll be fine.'

'What happened to Manzoni?' he asked.

'You shot him in the stomach. He

died a few hours later,' came the reply.

'So it's all over then?'

Renate's hand caressed his forehead.

'*Caro mio*,' she said softly. 'It's only just beginning.'

The door opened and Joe and Frankie entered the bedroom. When she saw Brad was awake, Frankie said, 'Joe's passed his exams, Sergeant Saunders. We're gonna be married here in Roberta with our parents' blessing.'

'See what I mean?' Renate said with a smile. 'And we are a family again, at last.'

THE END